The Facilitators

The Peter Redgrove Library

Other Peter Redgrove books available from Stride:

The Peter Redgrove Library:
1. *In the Country of the Skin*
2. *The Terrors of Dr. Treviles**
3. *The Glass Cottage**
4. *The God of Glass*
5. *The Sleep of the Great Hypnotist*
6. *The Beekeepers*
7. *The Facilitators*
8. *The Colour of Radio: Essays and Interviews*
[*with Penelope Shuttle]

The Laborators
Abyssophone
Orchard End
What the Black Mirror Saw
Sheen
A Singer for the Silver Goddess

A Curious Architecture [contributor]
Earth Ascending [contributor]

i.m. Peter Redgrove:
Full of Star's Dreaming: Peter Redgrove 1932-2003

The Facilitators
or Mister Hole-in-the-Day

A Novel

Peter Redgrove

The Facilitators
This edition 2006

ISBN 1-905024-14-2

Cover design by Neil Annat
Cover photos © Alistair Fitchett
Used with kind permission of the artist

The Peter Redgrove Library
is published by
Stride Publications
11 Sylvan Road, Exeter
Devon EX4 6EW
England

www.stridebooks.co.uk

Thanks

The Peter Redgrove Library is grateful to the following subscribers who have helped make the publication of these titles possible:

Cliff Ashcroft
Andrew Bailey
Martin Bax
Hazel Carruthers
Philip Fried
Mark Goodwin & Nikki Clayton
David Grubb
Michael Longley
Adrian & Celia Mitchell
Brian Louis Pearce
Malcolm Ritchie
Geoff Sutton & Bernard Gilhooly
Leonie Whitton & David Westby

to the following for help, encouragement and support in other ways:

Tony Frazer
Neil Roberts
Penelope Shuttle
the late Philip Hobsbaum

and to Arts Council England, South West for financial support.

Introduction

The experience of reading Peter Redgrove's work will – of course – be different for every reader, but may also be so for the same reader at different times. I first read *The Facilitators* in 1992, at a time when I had recently made contact with him and was publishing a small fraction of his poetry in the magazine I edited (*Memes*). I read it again, thirteen years later, in order to write this introduction and with the author two years deceased. The act of re-reading was just that, but also something more – an attempt at re-reading my initial reading, a sense of which somehow arose as I read, as well as a re-reading in the context of my continued engagement with Redgrove's work.

One passage, towards the end of the novel, came across – again – as being particularly significant, but all the more so after thirteen years' additional practice in the art of life. The narrator – one of several vying for the hand of the elusive Director of 'the mysterious Institute of Facilitation' – encounters three of her staff, all of whom are instructed to deny they are *not* her. Reacting against the sexual initiation they confer, collectively, upon him, he blurts out that 'I came looking for the explanation of a mystery'. To which the reply is, simply, 'We have shown you the mystery. There is no explanation of what happens when love is made'.

The Facilitators, as a whole, is not a book of explanations, but a vehicle that allows Redgrove to explore his key themes in a fresh context. And, as ever, it can't be said that one book ends where another begins – concepts and images recur, along with whole poems on occasions, and what we are presented with, therefore, is a monad that reflects the others.

The narrative (lightly-plotted as it is) allows concepts and insights to sneak beneath the skin in a way that, for certain readers, might not otherwise be the case. However, that isn't to downplay the beauty of the writing or the way in which it restates what, arguably, is Redgrove's key theme – the equivalence of the 'material' and the 'spiritual'. After the Platonic separation of reality into a spiritual realm and an inferior material one, and the subsequent death of belief in the former, Redgrove's work re-envisages matter in a 'spiritual' way. The language he uses reflects this process of re-*anima*-tion:

'So I caper with my left-hand bride in the great mud. We dance earth and water and the yeasty air and the reddening fire of the sun, which strikes smoky azures, mauves, crimsons, velvety blacks and vermilions from the watery mud . . .'

The bee, main symbol of the Institute's cult, is itself presented as a creature both 'material' and' spiritual' – a 'symbol of the art-ful busi-ness of the never-resting earth-spirit' – and this relates the book (first published in 1982) to certain occult trends of the time, as expressed in the work of Kenneth Grant and the American occultist Nema as well as in the music of occult-aware bands such as Killing Joke (a track on whose 1982 LP *Revelations* is entitled 'The Hum'). In particular, Grant's symbolic account of the bee, as the collector of the 'sexual honey' of the priestess in sex-magical ritual, is not only consistent with Redgrove's perspective as a truly magical materialist, but also suggests his (continuing) subversive potential. To remember Redgrove, after all, as some kind of cuddly English eccentric would be insulting – and, beyond the bouncy narrative of this book, there exists a world-view that is closer to the outlaw world-views of Grant, Crowley and Spare than to mainstream thought.

Redgrove, to his credit, has smuggled these concepts into wider parlance, in a way that these fringe operators have not, without diminishing their integrity in the least – so that the textual honey tempts the otherwise-sceptical reader, suggesting mysteries too sweet to explain. And re-reading this novel has reminded me, tangentially, of pollens gathered earlier in my own life – possibilities that remain, even now that the bomb culture of the Eighties and my own mid-twenties seem so distant, along with many others suggested by his vast and resonant Work.

Norman Jope

Dedicated in gratitude to the memory of Gerald Massey, master of facilitation through the reverie of languages; and to the Institutes of Facillitation, wherever they may first appear.

Peter Redgrove

Acknowledgments

Grateful acknowledgments are due to the BBC for the commissioned work in which certain of the themes of this novel were first rehearsed, as follows: *Jack Be Nimble* (BBC TV) produced by Michael Croucher; *Dance the Putrefact* (Radio 3) produced by David Spenser; *Martyr of the Hives* (Radio 4) produced by Brian Miller. The last of these won a Giles Cooper Award for Radio Drama 1981, and its text appears in *Best Radio Plays of 1980* (Eyre Methuen/BBC 1981).

There is a Moment in each Day that Satan cannot find
Nor can his Watch Fiends find it, but the Industrious find
This Moment & it multiply. & when it once is found
It renovates every Moment of the Day if rightly placed

Blake: *Milton* 35: 42-6

She had caused to be placed in the entrance hall, in an alcove, to the left of the big staircase, a life-sized bronze bust of Aristotle. She had arranged that a small jet of water should play over the head from above, making the curls and whiskers shine as though they had been anointed. She had also contrived that water should jet from beneath, as in a bidet, and should spurt through the hollow base and throat of the head to play on to the crown from within, making the bronze ring and whisper.

'Look,' she would say to her clients, 'here is a teacher. When I am not with you, when I am absent or too busy to see you, listen to the head. Bend to its lips and listen to the whisper of the water.' Often, when Madame could not be found, a queue would form to listen to the head. Sometimes scuffles occurred. Then she told us that the head would not speak to violent people, and neither would she. The violence passed like a cloud.

* * * * *

'She is the princess of a very curious kingdom. She has converted herself into a fairy-tale; she has made herself into a therapy. She has a marvellous smile, which is seldom seen. Consequently those of us on the outer fringe of her favours, compete for that smile. I have heard that the man who can make her laugh aloud will become her husband.'

'I consider myself neither client, nor patient, nor do I suffer from any tremor or illness. I have simply come in a mask, to marry her. The sun was shining through the great windows on to the glittering and bearded bust, like a golden half-smile under a caul of water. I walked straight up to the head, knocked on it, and bent my ear to its shimmering dribbling lips. I seemed to hear a distant voice, vibrating somewhere under the floor where the pipes ran, calling out "Beware . . . beware . . . "Over and above this deep note in the water a higher sound seemed to be singing: "Be mad for love, be mad for love . . ."

I straightened up. I would wear the mask of madness. I would put myself into this Doctor's care, and create a madness that would arouse not merely her professional curiosity, but her love as well. A madness to make a Good Doctor smile, or even laugh aloud!'

'We shall be married in the old police station which is now the registry office. After our wedding, we'll go back to my Institute, and we'll have drinks all together. Then I will shut the whole place down. I will turn off for ever the faucet that keeps Aristotle whispering tales into the ears of my patients. Derek will be there, and Donald; and Xavier too, cured of his frenzies; Daniel and Surtees. One of these men will in that hour have become my dear husband. Can you, I wonder, guess which one it will be?'

* * * * *

'I am Donald, or Derek. I am disturbed about the age of my ghost. The adventure began when I found that I could not prevent myself groaning in church. Now I wish to divorce my first wife, and marry an heiress. I would not stop at murder to accomplish this. I have considered my plans so often that they resemble memories.'

'I am Derek, or Donald. That is all the name I have, unless it be Opportunism, or Lechery. I have formed a plan. I shall pose as a client, or a patient, of the very rich Doctor who runs this Institute. I shall seduce her, and then marry her. Her name is music to me: Jacqueline Petula Dimitrios. We are matched, except for the matter of money; we both have every charm and grace. But, for myself, I believe in nothing. Nothing at all.'

'We are the female staff of the Institute, and our names are Julia, Jennie and Ann. We are instructed to deny we are not Madame. We hope soon to welcome Cecilia to our number, as we are a Sisterhood. These men! They chase after Madame for cure and healing, and their image is a wedding: happily ever after. They are like drones on their wedding-flight, like sleepy sperm jostling in great tufted beards of plasm. However, we have a great deal of housework that must be done, besides our duties to Madame's clients. So we keep alert. We reside in the cellar with our babies and the remains of the man we are instructed to deny is not our father.'

'I am Xavier. I have an interest in God, in Mud, and in my left-hand Wife. I believe I can taste with my whole skin, and sometimes that I can see through it. What is unreasonable about this? Are the eyes not hollowed skin, and do we not taste with the skin of our mouths? However, in my wish to explore and if possible develop these perceptions, I am liable to certain frenzies. I like this Institute, as the staff are instructed to indulge them. I believe Dr Dimitrios knows certain of the secrets of visionary taste-touch, and I would like to join her abilities to my own. This would mean marrying her.'

'I am Cecilia, and married to a certain client of Madame's. I have obtained an appointment to the staff of this Asylum or Institute as a nurse. My deeper purpose is, however, to keep my eye on my husband, and, if possible, to obtain a child from him. With his knowledge and consent, or without. I am instructed to indulge certain frenzies of the clients. I hope these intimacies and energies will not carry me along with them to love these other men too deeply.'

'I am a child of the Institute, still forming my plasm. Where I am is beset with echoes, which become visible, like dreams, and then I am sometimes a woman searching for her husband; sometimes a black man, very tall; sometimes I am married to Dr Dimitrios. Often a warmth swims into this place, and then I am nothing but a golden countenance, smiling under a caul.'

'I am Daniel. My hair is red as fire and I am four foot six inches in height. It is my pleasure to teach schoolchildren correct ways, and to assist in the jacuzzi. Though I am her masseur, I am not inclined towards Madame. I would, however, like to marry her, to ensure the proper administration of funds.'

'My name is Surtees Geoffrey, and I have become known as Sir Geoffrey, for short. I have learnt Beekeeping, and how to conduct my own affairs. I am also black, and have been appointed a member of staff. My dearest wish is to marry Madame, though I would that she were also black as night or the interior of my hives.'

'I am Jacqueline Petula Dimitrios, MD. I am one of the richest women in the world, and my husband, if I should choose one, would be one of the richest men. The problem is that I cannot put my millions to full use until I have discovered the consort who will make my riches meaningful. As they are all after me for my money here, I think that I will make the chase part of the cure.'

* * * * *

I have known Madame quite a long time, but at first it was on tape, and by accident. I was intrigued by an advertisement in the health magazine. Relaxation, it said, was the clue to living. Learn relaxation, and your blood-pressure will drop, your spots fade, superfluous hair drop out, manners become more graceful, suave, tranquil. I filled in the coupon and posted it off. When the padded envelope arrived a couple of weeks later, I was irritated to find that the firm, Thunderbolt Cassettes, Ltd, had posted me the wrong tape. I had requested the American spiel. I wanted a male American voice, down to earth, relaxed in itself. Also the Americans were usually first in the field with such gadget-aids to thought or reflection.

I had been sent instead a tape called *Relaxation for Serenity*, and the speaker was one Madame Dimitrios, hailing from the Institute of Facilitation, Rainmouth. I put the tape on. It ran for a few seconds silently, then I heard for the first time the voice that was to mean so much to me.

'I want you to settle comfortably in an armchair. Kick off your shoes, loosen any tie or belt. Simply listen to my voice, there is nothing else you have to do. Listen to what I say, and you will find that you are doing as I suggest, without thought, without effort. Allow this to happen, let go. Be sure you are perfectly comfortable. There must be no tension about the neck. Support your head with a small cushion. Now take some deep breaths. Let your stomach swell out as you breathe in. This means that you are using your lungs to their fullest extent, deep down. Breathe in . . . now out. In . . . out. In . . . out. Choose a spot on the wall a little higher than your normal gaze. Or a hairline crack, any mark. Let your attention flow between that mark and your eyes. Let it flow. Now remember sleep. Remember what happens each night of your life when you easily and simply fall asleep. Your eyes are heavy, you let them close. When you are tired your eyes are heavy and they close of themselves. It is a very pleasant feeling. As the eyelids drop, there is a little dislocation, a little disorientation, and relaxation begins to flow through the body. Allow this to happen, now. Allow your eyelids to remember this heaviness, sleepiness. You are going to sleep now, with heavy lids, but it is a special sleep. It is a waking sleep, and you will experience waking dreams. Your eyes, because you have reminded them of sleep, are flickering, closing. You swallow once, because you are so relaxed. And your eyes close. And your chin sinks. And you sink down.'

It was a pleasant surprise how easy it was to listen, to drift, and then to find it so totally natural to allow the eyelids to close of their own accord.

The tape continued, asking me to persuade my body to recollect further sensations of drowsiness, of sinking, of warmth, of heaviness. I found myself in a relaxed twilight state, and Madame Dimitrios's voice seemed exceptionally gentle and soft. Somebody dropped a piece of iron in the street, and the sound rang in my senses, as though my skin were a tranquil pool, and somebody had flung a stone in it. I felt pleasantly amused when what Madame suggested would begin to happen, did happen. She asked me to feel the warmth and weight of my right arm, and warmth and weight duly appeared in it. There should now be a tingling in the fingers, she said, and there was. So it was with my other arm, my legs, my whole body. Then I was to let that heaviness melt away, and sink down, and it did, and only a person-shaped warmth was left, floating, as she now suggested, and speeding over the green twilit landscapes, buoyed up on a white fleecy cloud that spread all around me, carrying me far, far away. As she spoke of this high and serene vehicle, I saw the picture she suggested in a flash, which faded, then reappeared, and I understood how the flashes would join up and become a steady condition. Which they did. I turned over and looked down between the soft tendrils of the moisture that supported me, then back again and up at the full moon that was riding high and sharp-edged in a sky full of stars.

The vision faded, and I was once again in my armchair, with Madame's persuasive and exquisite voice in my ears, murmuring that I must relax my brow and my neck, that my shoulders were being stroked by gentle warm hands, and were widening as they were stroked, and that relaxation was stealing over my face, which was settling into lines as harmonious as a Buddha's face. I saw or felt that tranquil smiling moonface laid over my own, or my own face dissolving into that smile, then I thought the tape suddenly changed direction, and began to address me personally.

'Listen. I am Madame Dimitrios and I am in the most deadly danger. I am held captive in this place by madmen and unless I sign my wealth over to them, they will kill me and train my twin sisters to take my place. I fasten this message at the centre of this hypnotic tape and send it out into the unknown, as I would seal a message into a bottle and cast it into the sea of sleep. It will I know somewhere, somehow survive, and be washed up on the shores of a waking consciousness, summoning bold rescuers.'

The voice faded into a watery babbling as I struggled awake, and into a whistling which ran down the scale as other words reformed: '. . . deeper and deeper relaxed with each outbreath . . . you are breathing along your bones, your long bones which are warming your breath which is warming your bones . . .' I snapped off the recorder and rubbed my eyes hard. Then I pressed the review button and listened to the tape again from the point where the instructions about relaxing the face began. I was careful to keep myself from dropping off as I re-ran them. The instructions continued in a perfectly orderly manner with relaxation of the scalp ('like warm oil pouring slowly under the hairline') and the back of the neck, the shoulders and the length of the spine imagined as possessing a tap fitted to its base: turn the tap and all tensions drained away from the body into the earth's centre. Immediately after this the voice went on to give directions about breathing through one's long bones, which was where I came in, or tumbled out.

Was there something in the tone of voice that communicated such a message of panic, which my subliminal mind, alerted by the relaxation, was able to decode? Obviously I had fallen asleep and dreamed this message of a damsel in distress, but was it only my dream? Or perhaps there was a message overrecorded on top of the manifest instructions, which my ears could only hear in the sensitivity of the hypnoidal state.

I did not favour the last conjecture, for as I experimented with the tape, though I always (provided I allowed myself to slip into the sleeping awareness) heard similar messages, sometimes it was a dragon I had to rescue her from, and once an immense spider, like Miss Muffet; sometimes a wicked witch, and at others the seven dwarves. I concluded that the effect of the relaxation procedure was to expose in my own psyche this urgency; something provoked by the tape was calling out inside me for rescue. Well, I thought, we all need rescue one way or another: Dr Dimitrios as much as another. The tape uncovered resonances. We are full of little gods, unborn children, aborted selves, ghosts of various ages. But I resolved that I would find this woman Dimitrios and discover whether her presence would shed light on these ingenious appeals. Also, I wondered how many of these tapes had been published, and whether they had a similar effect on all their listeners. Then I looked up Dr Jacqueline Petula in the reference books, learnt of her beauty and immense wealth, and resolved to make our marriage my life-work.

* * * * *

It could have been a hundred years later that I woke from a doze and found myself in the pleasant day-room of the Institute. As one does on waking, I looked around inside myself to see what accustomed discomforts and worries were active today. I was delighted to encounter a pleasant interior silence. I felt exactly as relaxed and alert as if I had just finished playing my cassette of Madame. But then I remembered where I was and who I was, and the whole train of recollection and resolution came into view. How could I have forgotten, even in sleeping? I had duly presented myself as a patient, or client, and all else had been forgotten, for an indeterminate time, like an enchantment. I had become so wrapped up in my prepared story of neurosis, of habits of anxiety and agitation, of haunted tape-recorders and overweening compulsions, that everything else but the details of my fiction had vanished! Now I woke up to find that I had joined Madame's Institute and, for how long a time I did not know, had forgotten my purpose in doing so. It was time to begin! My priority must be to seek an interview with the Director, without delay.

I pushed my way up out of the very comfortable and over-relaxing winged armchair where I had been rapt, and walked across the soft and silent carpet to the entrance, beyond which lay the hall and the administrative offices. On the way I passed the big man we knew as Sir Geoffrey. He was naked as usual, and sitting in front of a large coffee-table on which were spread several sheets of paper. He was writing on them, but invisibly, as I had already discovered. It was the eccentricity of this distinguished knight to soothe his overworked mind by writing out documents with a fountain-pen filled with some kind of plain water. It was no doubt a relaxation from his business-life, which must have proved over-arduous. This compromise, I imagined, would not tax his mind, nor in effecting it would he have to break the continuity of such valuable habits as, for example, minuting board-room conversations and other meetings; but here he did it with a clear nib. We had grown friendly, but today I felt suddenly irritated by his compulsion. I stopped, and looked over his shoulder.

'Sir Geoffrey,' I said, 'has it never occurred to you that it is foolish, exceedingly foolish, to write messages to yourself that neither you nor any other can ever read? Pull yourself together, man! Snap out of it!'

Sir Geoffrey slowly turned to me, gathering in his papers, got up, and smiled. He laid his hand heavily on my shoulder, towering over me, and led me over to the log-fire that blazed in the big hearth at the end of the room. We knelt down together in front of it, and he held up his blank sheets of paper to the warm blaze. Slowly jet-black writing appeared on the hitherto blank pages, gradually manifesting itself in oblique strokes, broad and fuzzy, covering the white paper made crisp and crinkly as banknotes by the heat.

'How do you do it?' I whispered. He picked up his gold Parker pen and tapped it with a fingernail.

'I fill it with tapwater and piss,' he said, 'every morning. I write what I have dreamt, or my new-waking thoughts, with that night's distillation. I record the body's invisible tales in the body's invisible ink. I cannot falsify as I write because I cannot read back what I have written. When the evening fire is lighted I develop the night's photographs in front of it, in preparation for the new night's work.' He winked. There was a lot of winking done in that Institute, I thought crossly, not entirely satisfied by the madman's explanations for his piss-play. The wink was intended to imply friendly complicity and helpfulness; there was a special neologism that was used to dignify this custom. It was an ugly one: 'Facilitation'; but I could hardly conceal my disgust. To me his too-juicy wink communicated a horrible naivety of welcome, as to some vivid feast of unnatural food.

* * * * *

Sir Geoffrey winked, and handed me a portion of the sheaf of papers. He watched me examine them, with an amused smile. I couldn't help sniffing at the black script. The pages were crisp and crinkly, and smelt pleasantly of nothing worse than the heat and the coal fire. Now I read what was written there, as Sir Geoffrey got up and softly walked away on bare feet.

DREAM-KIT

Shut away here in Rainwall
With these provocative black
Materialising cabinets: TV or radio set,

That raise horrors and slight
Glories in the mind with
Invisible rhythms caught in

Their lightless black interiors
On skeletal fingers. The whole
Earth's atmosphere is a pond

Of trembling waves made
Of invisible colours, a river
Of transmission full of

Coloured images of where it's been,
Its receptive water peering into cities
Full of troubling troubled ripples

The news makes and the dramatists
And the rainbowing commercials, and packed
With invisible creatures that swim

Plainly into view on the
Aquarium of your screen.
The set itself is like the window

On to a great tank of sharks,
Or one set into a swimming-pool,
Or into a river's banks,

You switch from place to place,
You have so many windows: it is like
A diving-bell searching over ooze

Or a tumbler pushed into a stream for you to see
The sportive minnows footballing
Back and forth over the green watery colours:

But they are all phantasms: you are watching
Vibrations only, rhythms, which are
Nothing shaking the radio-ether, which is

Nothing also. Racks and racks
Of goodly looking nothing in a broadcasting hypermarket
Transmitting centuries of miles away,

And not at that moment either
Since these are only phantasms of reflections
Stored on tape, strips of plastic

Lined with finely powdered forms of rust.
And these rays penetrate our brains,
Like God's rays of outer space

That warm us, but unlike those
Asking only that we remain
Distracted. The TV set

Is an artificial dreaming-kit.
The true instrument
Is the dreaming mind

That pushes its tumbler
Into the river that flows
Under the skin: the groping

Caressing fingers enter
The neck's skin and grasp words there
That cry out.

* * * * *

There were certain seed-facts at that Institute. I call them seed-facts because they were in the air, floating, like a zest, possibly from the breath of any people there who had discovered their way to well-being; or from those who, being unable to discard their habitual symptoms for the time being, lived by not paying excessive attention to them; or from those who were simply in a mental ferment. As I remember, the only torpid patients I saw were those who had just arrived, and had not yet found their feet in the Institute.

I thought of these data as seeds of a metaphysical tree. They took root in their own manner, like the biblical grain of mustard-seed. Before you knew it there was a great tree bending limber to the wind, and strong enough to bear its burdens of interpretation, as the lithe spine of a man bears his weighty head. This tree, I felt, announced its flowering by a certain perfume in the mind.

The notion of 'Facilitation' was one of these seeds. An ugly word. I learnt it in conversation with the personage who helped me with my trunk when I arrived, which was an aluminium chest full of books, white shirts, and my Morris-dancing equipment. He couldn't have been more than four foot six high. As he pushed through the baize swing-door in the stairs I took him for a tubby urchin. He wore a denim cap with a big peak which hid his face. For a while I imagined I was being helped by a strong child rather than a pituitary dwarf.

We paused on the landing. He took his cap off and wiped his brow with the back of his hand. As he did this he revealed his close-cropped red hair, which gave me a shock. It was like a wound, as though the top of his head had been taken off, or as if he had been freshly scalped. The head and face were the size of an adult man, but the body and limbs were those of a perfectly proportioned child. As he stood smiling at me without a trace of embarrassment, and I doing my best to conceal mine, it was difficult to see head and body joined together to make one personality. The face was too large, the fingers too exquisitely small, to belong to the one person. That adult head had borrowed the skin of the child's body, for the face was hardly lined, ruddy and fresh and glowing with health. But there were crowsfeet at the eyes' corners, and I estimated that he was in his early forties. As we stood there with polite smiles, sizing each other up, my back gave a twinge of pain in sympathy with the disparity between our sizes.

'I'd better be careful. This back of mine is apt to go into spasm.'

The man-boy laughed.

'Don't worry about it. I'll be your facilitator.'

'My *what?*'

'I'll facilitate your back.'

'You mean make it better. Are you one of the doctors?'

'Oh, don't use that word. Facilitators. I'll not cure your back. I'll facilitate it to get better. I will give it permission to cure itself.'

'What an ugly word, if you don't mind my saying so.'

'That's all right. But it's a beautiful concept.'

'Are you an authority on backs?'

'Let's get your box upstairs.'

I grasped the leather handle on my side and watched how the urchin opposite lifted his. When he did so by bending his knees and straightening them rather than hoisting with bent back, I followed suit. The trunk seemed light. It was easy to get it up the remaining stairs and down the quiet corridor to my room. I had the impression that the dwarf could have lifted and carried it by himself, without difficulty. We put the trunk on a luggage-rack at the end of the double bed. I thought I should find out more about the dwarf's status before I offered him a tip.

'What do you do here?'

'I look after the baths and massage. I teach yoga.'

'You're the physiotherapeutic facilitator.'

As I spoke, he took off his cap again, and looked hard at me. I regretted that I had spoken ironically. Then he gave me an enormous wink, puckering up his eye and releasing it like somebody blowing a kiss.

'Daniels. Dan Daniels. Call me Dan. I hope you'll come to me for some hydrotherapeutic work. Then we can see to that back.'

I knew from the advertisement that they had devices and treatments here for all manner of ills; very nearly fifty-seven varieties of bath; mud-baths, peat-baths, seaweed, oatmeal (did that mean porridge baths?), pine and sitz baths, and for all I knew toast and marmalade or egg and bacon baths. I wondered what a sitz bath was. I felt I wanted one before I left.

Daniels turned his back on me to leave. Then his head swung round and he winked at me again. I found people did wink a lot here. A wink was an elementary facilitation, implying blanket approval and permission. When he had gone, I tried out various kinds of wink in the mirror. I rehearsed Dan's cheerful departing wink, amazed at how far round over his shoulder the little fellow was able to turn his head.

* * * * *

An idea that was very much in the air of the Institute was that of the reality of imaginative experience. I nearly said 'trance experience', but that gives too extreme a picture of sibylline utterance, or bombazine mediums sprawling with snoring mouths and exuding ectoplasm, sago'ed with tiny spirit faces, all over their Queen Mary bosoms. The simple attention one gives to a story vividly told; the relaxation of watching a coal-fire or a snowfall, and the pictures that arise in one's mind as one does so; the trance of concentration when one is performing a complicated but congenial task, such as screwing gently – all these are more than simple physical gratification, and were seen here to be a continuum with the extreme states; such as an abreaction on the analyst's couch, well-nigh hallucinating in an ecstasy of recollection; the epileptic fit ushered in with coloured lights and other auras; the man in the grip of an obsessive-compulsive act, acting out the images and symbols of some concealed trauma; or indeed the mediumistic utterance. I could not have predicted the dedication with which this Institute subscribed to the actuality and realisation of this view.

* * * * *

Sir Geoffrey facilitated me towards his own view of urine. I read his piss-poem thoughtfully. The means by which he concealed the work from himself until it was ready to display itself as a whole before the roaring common-room fire, was an interesting comment on the process of artistic creativity. I read the poem for the umpteenth time, drinking coffee. I got up and went to the loo because my bladder was full. As I stood there urinating, I ruminated on the poem, in my memory. The used coffee passed out of me, and as it did so, my body relaxed. In my relaxation, almost as though I were in a mild trance, the images of the poem paced towards me, and its focus grew sharper. I found I could see it as a whole, and the argument was plain. Why, television and radio were a substitute for inner theatre, most especially a substitute for dreaming. And now, I was in a sort of piss-dream, pissing dreamily, relaxed, satisfied. I considered my posture. How stable it was, feet planted firmly a little apart, my centre of gravity low, and my head bowed contemplating my root, an odour which was one of the signatures of existence wafting up. It was a contemplative pose, and I was contemplating. I considered Rodin's 'The Thinker'. Did he not appear to be contemplating by his backward route?

The Institute's seed-facts were germinating. I had already, for the second time since my arrival, forgotten my purpose in coming here. Why, I was on a deceitful expedition to marry a very rich woman, and no doubt I should and would lie and cheat to the best of my ability to get her and win my fortune. Yet, just a moment, would I not lie most convincingly if I cultivated a temporarily self-deceiving trance of sincerity, like a child swearing to a tale it knows is not true? Had I not begun to learn techniques of this kind with the relaxation-tape, and its trance that was ambiguous, since a listener was rendered unable to decide whether it was his own mind he was listening to, or Madame's? Was it that he was overcome by deep levels of his own mind, or was he possessed by another's intentions; raped by his own spirit, or by another's? Here at the Institute, I thought, it hardly mattered; the atmosphere of facilitation and the readiness to respond open-heartedly to whatever came from that, accounted for the wonderful sense of energy in the air. If I held to my purpose.

Sir Geoffrey had facilitated a fresh attitude in me. The Bible said that it was the neglected and forgotten boulder that was made the cornerstone of the building. Because Sir Geoffrey was, quite literally, a dirty old man, did that necessarily make him wrong-headed? He must have a very young spirit to be interested in such a discovery; or was it that his ghost was much older than those of other men, and to that extent more knowledgeable about neglected matters? I wondered how old my own ghost was.

* * * * *

I still do not know whether the materialisation seance was a fake. I came down early one morning to find a new notice pinned up on the board by the whispering head: MADAME DIMITRIOS WILL HOLD A SEANCE TONIGHT IN THE BILLIARD-ROOM. Underneath in smaller letters were the words *Materialisations anticipated.*

The overhead lights of the big billiard-table blazed from its green baize. People were gathering among the armchairs, which were drawn up in the shadows of the room, all facing the left-hand corner by the hearth. This corner had been fitted with a brass rail with heavy rings to which were fastened velour drapes. When the curtains were drawn close it would make a tall, thin triangular cabinet like a prism on its end. Two men were struggling to fit a large wooden carved throne into this space. By the time the arrangements were completed, we had all found places, and were waiting in anticipation, the two assistants standing quietly on each side of the throne wedged in the curtained corner. The large winged armchair next to me on the right was empty.

A shaft of light struck into the semi-darkness as the door opened at the back of the room. A tall figure walked quickly between the armchairs and stood facing the curtained space, holding itself very upright. Her long dress was darkness itself, and from the back she seemed hooded in her long dark hair. Then she turned, and the black veil covering her entire head revealed only the glimmer of a face and the blurred sketch of a mouth. She had been holding her breath, for when she let it out in a long sigh, there was the shimmer of a smile behind her veil as it fluttered; at that sigh or that smile everybody in the room relaxed.

Madame sat down on the throne inside the curtained cabinet. The two assistants came forward and tied her wrists and ankles to the throne with darkly coloured handkerchiefs. This done, the two took hold of the curtain-folds on either side, and paused, evidently waiting for permission to draw them. Madame began to speak then, and for the first time I heard in the flesh the voice I knew so well from my relaxation-tape, which I had played I don't know how many times, over and over. I could turn on the recording instrument between my ears, and hear that voice in my skull speaking its terrified messages of relaxation. The ferro-magnetic ghost had spoken through the body of a machine; I had made it speak also within the chamber of my own head, and there had obeyed it; now it was uttering as though it might turn up at any time and at any place, unchanged, but in this instance from the mouth of a veiled shadow inside a curtained box. She-who-hides, I thought, She-who-hides.

'My friends here have tied me to make me passive and to guard against fraud. I ask you, my students and fellow-facilitators, to ask yourselves if there can in this case be fraud. Whether it is the spirits that act or I myself that cause the phenomena, either is a form of story-telling. You cannot decide such questions, and should therefore not allow them to divert you from the experience. I am not the medium but the facilitator. Or, I put the warning into another form, you should not be afraid, or allow that fear to close your senses. I shall ask one of my assistants to light this small red-shaded oil lamp on the table, and this will be the only light, as my other assistant will switch off the electricity at the mains. Is this to guard against the discovery of fraud? Or is it because there is a risk of light falling upon the sensitive ectoplasm with which the spirits make their temporary bodies, snapping it back into my body like bruising elastic and causing an internal haemorrhage? I will not decide this question for you. But I ask you again to guard against fear. Fear shapes the exudations of our collective mind into abominable shapes. We sweat chemical substances which, (depending on your hypothesis) either enter our relaxed concentration and cause bad dreams, or taint the thirsty ectoplasm like sour milk. Remember how the angel spoke to Mary, and the Word conceived in her womb. You must think of your devoted facilitator pregnant with the dreams and personal secrets you have told me. Regard this seance as a communication concerning these secrets, whether mediated by my unconscious mind, or by some discarnate spirit. You will note how my legs are fastened wide apart to the legs of this chair. You must not conjecture whether I slip my bonds and walk around in this dark room invisible in my black dress and veil, or whether tacky mind-stuff pours from my womb and is shaped with limbs and life and volition and a veil, as it might be a ghostly daughter wandering among you, gripping a wax candle in her transparent fist, shaped by my unconscious mind from my womb, just as the incarnate child is formed by the same organ in ceaseless building during its accustomed nine months. Nor do you know whether this introduction itself spoken by me is a barker's spiel calculated to raise phantoms of suggestion in your minds. Do not conjecture. Think of it as Japanese theatre. Ghosts and spirits walk the stage. Theatre originated in temple mediumship; the operatic itself is nothing but vehement sheer possession.'

Madame ceased speaking, the brass rings of the curtains swept across with a rattle as of tambourines, and the lights went out. Gradually the faint red glow from the little oil lamp reached into our eyes as their round curtains opened, and I felt a cool hand steal into my own.

This was interesting! Naturally I had surveyed the field. I did not intend my pursuit of Madame within the confines of this Institute to be single-minded or celibate. I had looked them over, the female patients, my fellow-facilitators, and looked the staff over too. There was one slender nurse, but she appeared only at mealtimes and was Xavier's facilitator. As she sat at table, I could not distinguish her charms beneath the faceful of custard. But so far I had made no moves. I was delighted that somebody had taken an independent decision about me, under the cover of the dark. An atmosphere of ghostly terror was a delicious stimulant, hence the popularity of horrorfilms. The more violent the film, the tighter the girlfriend's grip. Instructed not to fear, we would instead take comfort in companionship. I was glad the curtain was drawn, and we were invisible to Madame, and she to us. I gave the hand an encouraging squeeze. I tried to make out the appearance of my new friend, but in the dim red glow I could only just glimpse a shadowing within the shadowy armchair.

My hand-squeeze was returned. I cursed my previous self-absorption, and wished I had seen whoever it was slip into the chair. I did not want to commit myself too far without knowing more about this pleasant neighbour. I squeezed again, and felt the little bones ripple in the warm hand. The hand felt young, yet an old woman's hand can be voluptuously flower-soft if there are no knobbly arthritic joints to give the age away. I did not think that an old person would reach out quite so swiftly for a youngish man's hand in the dark. I took my decision, and moved our clasped hands down from the arm of my chair to my knee, and, after a pause, from thence to my groin, risking all, for the excitement of the situation had begun to exert its bodily effects. Something other than Madame was sitting erect on the throne in its corner behind trouser-curtains. Suddenly the stranger hand loosed itself from my light grip, and squeezed me reassuringly in my important place. It felt for the tab and gently, gently unzipped my fly, glided its way as one accustomed to such intricacies, through the double opening of my trousers and underpants, found my bare skin, and gripped firmly the nude pillar rooted there.

It squeezed me reassuringly again, and then began to knead gently. A sudden image of my mother popped, most unexpectedly, into my mind. I saw her kneading dough for breadmaking. Then I could taste the crust of the warm loaf and touch the warmth of its sweet fluffy interior, with the faint flavour of alcohol from the yeast, no more than a zest. Warmth spread over my thighs and belly, and little shivers ran up my spine, like the resonance of a bass string on a cello. I was sinking down, deeply relaxed, and again I was reminded of Madame's voice on the tape, and wished she were doing this, adding the touch of her hand to the touch of her voice, which had reached right past my face into my mind; these fingers were achieving a complementary effect. There was relaxation and tension at once in my whole skin. It became so sensitive that in my trance of pleasure I fancied I could see the shape of the hand that was gently, slowly and lovingly bringing me to a delicious climax. I heard as it were from far away a species of rattling snore from behind Madame's curtain, but I was too far gone to pay attention. I was more concerned with what was accelerando materialising in my own secret corner.

Then I manifested. I was caught up by that indescribable sensation which is like something seen and tasted because it is touched. Two little pumps were beating happily inside, one at the back, one at the front, nether bellows, Cupid's wings flaring and beating. I must have been holding my breath during the last seconds of my concentration, my attention to the rising spirits at my very centre, my concentration, for I let out a loud shuddering sigh. It was like Madame's sigh at the beginning of the seance. I felt sure that if any of the audience heard, they would mistake it for Madame, or ghosts. My ectoplasmic rod was collapsing into the warm wetness it had materialised. I felt exceedingly happy, chirpy. How excellent when palm raises plasm mutating to psalm. I was not concerned overmuch about revealing visible sign of my activities; my trousers were dark as the medium's shadows, as her dress; such polite concerns hardly touched the peace that welled up in me. As I opened my eyes I seemed to glimpse a white shadow slipping back between the curtains of the cabinet. I craned round and tried again to see my lover, but the armchair appeared to be vacant. I stretched out and reached around in it, but she was gone. She? I had no certainty that it was a she. It could have been the redhaired dwarf for all I knew, with his delicate little hands.

I wondered what ghostly dramatics had been enacted all around us while my own ghost was being raised; my own white shadow slipping into that elusive sweet hand. At that moment the lights came on, and I put my hand up in front of my eyes. The curtain-rings jangled and there was Madame on her throne being untied. She stood up, and gave a loud slow sigh, which shuddered as mine had. Was this some mockery? Then she bowed to us. We struggled to our feet, and bowed back, except for half a dozen or so people who appeared to be soundly asleep. Then she stepped down out of the materialisation cabinet and walked past me again between the chairs.

A smile still hovered like some desirable fish below the shadowing of her veil; she carried an atmosphere with her like that faint zest of yeast of new bread. She wore an elbow-length black velvet glove on her right hand. I had noticed these gloves as the assistants fastened her clothed wrists to the throne. Now she was walking free, she held her left fist naked and doubled up; I saw it as she passed me. A doubt irritated my mind, and I stooped to hunt under the vacant armchair to my right for Madame's missing glove. But I found nothing to prove who my visitor had been either way. Now most of the audience had wended their way out. Five of the men remained: we were Xavier, Donald, Derek, Dan, and Sir Geoffrey. We all seemed reluctant to get up. I knew why I was reluctant. I was worried that the wetness on my trousers would after all shine out like a phosphorescent beacon to the others, who would guess immediately what had happened, and condemn me. Averting our gazes from each other, we silently rose, and politely filed from the room. I wondered what the others had experienced during the seance.

* * * * *

After my experience at the seance, I found it difficult to recover the composure I needed for my plans. I could not believe that I had been masturbated by the Director of the clinic, so thoroughly facilitated by this stranger, if it were she, cunningly slipping her bonds, and gliding from her curtained cabinet in spirit guise. Why, this would pre-empt our marriage, our consummation, my ambitions! And if it were a story told to me by my own mind, then I was fully entitled to lodge in this or any other loony-bin, and my intentions were manifest self-deception after all. Was this all they were?

The incident showed, if nothing else, that I was on a collision course with the object of my desire. The riches I desired were perhaps but a metaphor for the erotic treatment I hoped for from her and expected subliminally; or she from me. Or was it that the treatment I had received or imagined (for the psalmodic whisper into the palm had left no residue of plasm) was closer, much closer, to what I, and everybody else in this Institute, desired and desperately needed from their Great Facilitator, Madame? For one thing, if my fever to be the great Seducer were self-deception, and cold-hearted illusion, then the pronounced intimacy of this experience was strongly therapeutic. I felt warmth in my heart for the pleasure I had received, and a fondness for the room where I had received it, green baize, whitebeam cues and all, as I would remember a room in which I had been married. But the warmth was succeeded by a superstitious chill. If the seance was genuine, then what had masturbated me? If it were the ectoplasmic glove of a spirit, and spirits could be in many places at once, then what was to prevent its multiplying its gentle white hands? Hands only. After all, I had seen nothing, and felt only hand. Theoretically there was nothing to prevent everybody in the room from enjoying simultaneously an identical spirit hand in their trousers. Or up their skirt. The monstrous thought made me shudder. No reason — except the impossibility of such a mass fondling. Then my thoughts turned again. I had loved what had happened! I would not persuade myself to deny that. And if she had raised such an interesting ghost, skilled in imparting spiritual sensation, then it was an act of sharing and communion with everybody in the room, just as much as eating a small white flavourless host was, or more so, among so many.

Madame had specifically warned us against the type of self-debating I was now indulging. I decided to stop, now. Only, I did ask my friend, Sir Geoffrey, what he had seen at the seance.

'Oh, nothing,' he said, 'or nothing more than usual. I did my automatic writing. I always do on these occasions. I chose one of the armchairs with wings and a big armrest, laid out my pen and paper, and drifted off. I can always tell by smell when the paper's been used, though of course I can't read it. I wrote a good deal this time. It's just as though a hand other than one's own takes hold of one's pen. Would you like to come with me and develop the pages?'

I said I certainly would, so we went off together.

* * * * *

I had arrived that morning. It was a long journey and I was famished. A sign said 'refectory'. I looked through the glass panels of the swing doors and saw a couple of white-clad domestics spreading tablecloths across the broad elm boards and fetching from a sideboard huge foil-covered ceramic bowls. They set these at even distances along the centre-lines of the three big tables, three bowls on each. I tried the doors. They were locked.

A very little man with flaming red hair came along the corridor. He winked at me.

'Lunch is at twelve-thirty,' he said; 'come and sit down in the common-room until then.'

'Thanks. I will.' I pointed through the window. 'What are those?' The little man took an astonishing leap. It was monkey-like, that bound. He seemed to grip the flagstone floor with his toes so hard that they sent him bouncing upwards so he could peep through the glass.

'Those bowls? Why, they are famous. They were made specially for us at Prinknash. They are bowls of honey. You must meet our beekeeper. He is a fearless black man who never wears clothes.'

'Not even when he is beekeeping?'

'Oh, especially not then. The bees adore him. They walk over his skin, which shines with his exertions, looking at themselves in it, licking up his sweat. They regard his blackness as the throat of some infinite honey-flower, I guess. I have seen him covered with bees, bathing in them. Madame taught him. They went into the bee-garden together naked. Poor innocent, he went trusting, he knew nothing. Madame took the top off one hive, lifted out one of the frames crawling with bees, held it above his head, and shook the bees like pips all over him, while he stood there unprotesting. Perhaps because he was innocent, no harm came to him, not a bite, not a sting. That is how she made him beemaster. She is the only woman beemaster there has ever been. Ordinarily women can work with bees for only two weeks in a month. The smell of their ovulation or their menstruation drives the bees mad, infuriates them just as if you approached the hives with scented lotion on your hair. Madame has — some control. Pregnant women are more successful. You'd expect that. With that great hive of their own fastened to their bellies. Few care to try it.'

'How do elderly women fare?'

'Madame Dimitrios is ageless. That is not I think the explanation.'

'She is clearly a remarkable woman. When shall I meet her?'

The little man looked uneasy. 'There are a lot of patients here . . .'

'Yes, but surely, as a new arrival . . .'

'Oh, of course. But there will be some delay. Have you tried listening to the Bronze? This is recommended if treatment is delayed.'

'But am I likely to be treated by Madame herself?'

'Her very presence facilitates treatment.'

'She is not away, then?'

'Oh no, she is always present among us all.'

* * * * *

Warmed in front of the fire, the great furry, buzzing script duly developed, and Sir Geoffrey seemed very pleased with what he found. I felt restless still, after the seance. Was it time to have that sitz bath, or perhaps join the Aikido class? I had been there three full days already, and had initiated none of my plan. I was still waiting for my first interview with Madame. I wanted to see her face to face, without that veil. Then the incident in the seance-room came rushing at me again, and my mouth went dry, and tasted metallic.

If there were experiences like that available at the Institute, then I had better go slowly and carefully. And if the experiences were not the Institute's, but somehow my own unconscious installation, then I must be even more wary.

I wandered out into the lobby. There was a list of appointments with various members of staff posted on the notice-board, but none were scheduled with Dr Dimitrios. I assumed that they were ad hoc, and one was summoned. A notebook on a piece of string was provided, and one could write one's name in this for an appointment with a doctor. Printed on its cover was this injunction: VISIT FIRST THE BRONZE FACILITATOR. I thought I would.

The bronze head whispered away in its marble basin. The air around it was cool and fresh from the water that poured in a pleated veil over the sculpted curls and down the full beard. I liked the work; it was a copy of some Greek masterpiece of pre-classical times; it was too compassionate to be Aristotle. The head was set a little above chest-level. I leant towards the glittering lips and heard more clearly the sound of the water within the head. It was a low susurration combined with a slight and constant ringing as though the water had set the metal chiming with its soft pressure. As I tried to catch the faraway note of this sound, the sibilant water-murmur approached; but on the contrary when I concentrated on the sound of the water, the faint ringing, like rain on a metal roof, became clearer. I bent to the lips with a patient feeling, politely, as if trying to make out the feeble words of some aged relative. Ah, my relaxed attention was indeed forming words in the murmur! It was good psychology to place this head here like a fountain from which anybody could drink, providing they relaxed first! I knocked on the head. It said faintly, very faintly, *How old is your ghost?*

I straightened up, taken aback at the clarity of the faint words. I put my ear to the slightly parted lips again, listening. All I could hear was the water, and the faint ringing. No more words would come, neither re-statement nor explanation.

* * * * *

A short, hard-looking man with dull red hair spoke first.

'Of course we're very much against psychosurgery.'

His name was Daniels, and he was the Director today. He was talking to his lady visitor, a Dr Caecelia, in his sunny office on the third floor.

'If you'll allow me to use the expression, all loony-bins work, if they do work, by trying to get the loonies interested in life again. If you're not a coward, madness is the interesting thing. Most doctors are cowards, because they're so busy codifying anaesthesia, which they call normality. Madness is a feeling thing; the trouble is that normals tell the mad ones that what they are feeling is unreal, so the experiences are denied and replaced by symbolisations, which the normals triumphantly point to and call 'hallucinations".'

'It's all in Blake, if true,' says the lady, sagely. She touches her hair and brings a lock of it to her nostrils. It smells of honey.

'I could never understand a word of Blake . . .' says Daniels, '. . . so what we try to do is to turn the symbolisations back into experiences again. We like to act out.'

'But that is strictly forbidden,' says Dr Caecilia. She is recalling how Xavier, her special charge, inverted the great bowl of honey over her head this morning, and how it slipped down over her face like a gauzy caul, or a lazy caress.

'But then everything works of itself,' smiles Daniels. 'We

wish the images to flow freely. If they flow, we find there is no violence.'

'Do the fantasies export when clients come to rejoin the outer world?'

'We don't use that term "fantasy". Call it imagination, enthusiastic imagination. Well of course they adjust. They have a quest, you see. They have an understanding of that little piece of irreducible irrationality that is the core of any human being. Understanding it, they possess it; it does not possess them. It is irrepressibly creative. Many patients return here for a spell as members of staff. We call them "Facilitators".'

'There are several hypnotic devices scattered about the Institute. Like the whispering head.' Warm porridge in the face was more like being kissed by a hippopotamus than anything else, she thought; not unpleasant, really; one could eat the kiss.

'No, I'm afraid the word "hypnosis" won't do either. We have seeded the air with a few ideas, a few tapes, we have placed occasional emblems of power in our rooms and courtyards. Our clients will indeed add their own symbols, which were once their illnesses, their obsessions or hallucinations, and allow them to react. For the lucky ones, any object or person may open up depths to them. They are blissful, and difficult to control, but never violent.'

Caecilia wondered what murderous impulse Xavier was transmuting into comic transgressions, comic anointings; what parental forced-feeding. Really, he was the gentlest of men, provided one did not wear one's best uniform. Caecilia knew that Xavier had a greater thing planned than slapstick, to which it all tended, and wondered if she was to be involved. Their relationship had made an excellent step forward at the evening meal yesterday, when she had returned Xavier's custard with her cream jelly.

'You make them sound like poets,' she said.

'Few poets have gone as far,' pronounced Daniels, cheerfully.

'Who is Madame?' asked Caecilia. Daniels looked down at his hands.

'She is our Founder.'

'I loved the way that black chap simpered and called you "Madame".'

'He sees her everywhere,' said Daniels, pleased that Caecilia remembered the incident. He simpered. When his visitor had gone, he took out of a small conical cabinet, carved like a beehive, a clockwork mechanism with a battery-light in it and several mirrors on hinges, which he unfolded into a wheel. He wound up the little machine, (like the office, it was his for the day) and watched the whirling mirrors and listened to the deep hum the contrivance emitted. Soon his eyelids dropped. 'This is the Key of the Kingdom,' sang his sleeping face, and in his relaxation he took himself down through the narrow streets and the weedy lane to the house with the empty bed where he picked up the basket of moist flowers and buried his face in it. His simper widened and became a beautiful smile, and when he raised her face she was Madame. She went across to the dressing-table, sat down, and took a lipstick out of a drawer. She uncapped it, making as she did so a curious fanning gesture in front of the mirror; partly a movement of surprise with a hint of rejection, then, more rapidly, like brushing cobwebs or rubbing away smears on a windowpane so as to see through clearly. She stopped, she breathed deeply, and gave an enormous relaxed sigh, and then with bold fast strokes, put her lips on for the Disco.

* * * * *

The bee-lore in the Institute library was extensive. There I learnt that the ancient world regarded bees as spiritual beings. In the hierarchy of existence they lay somewhere between the plant-world and the animals, like plants that could hum and fly and build. Their spiritual function was that they mediated between the world-simple rhythm of growth-and-decline of the seasons, and the animals and human beings whose lives were spent in striving with that same environment. The rituals and religions of the animal-worshippers were marked by a ferocious blood-thirstiness and terrible blood-sacrifices; but sacrifices to the earth-goddesses were made with relenting honey. The bee was a symbol of the art-ful busi-ness of the never-resting earth-spirit. As for their humming, it was traditionally the sound made by the dead as they sported in the Elysian fields, most especially when they were occupied with the act of resurrection. Its sound was heard at the climax of the Orphic mysteries; it was the sound of rebirth and initiation, and if it were vibrated correctly by the expert yogin, then he would pass into a trance of surpassing knowledge. It was the sound of sounds, and some maintained that apprehending it was the natural consequence of the adept's learning to live at a high rate of vibration, when all ordinary sounds would slow down and weave together into the music of the spheres.

The library kept a book of newspaper cuttings that followed the Institute's history. The original founder was David Dimitrios. He had formed a Cult of the Bees, which had attained some notoriety, sufficiently so that when he was blown to pieces in a terrorist plot,* the colour supplements ran articles about him. There were pictures of him in plenty — a fit-looking old man of anything between sixty and eighty, with long white hair that escaped from the skullcap of the bee-uniform they all wore like steam from under the lid of a pot. He alone sported, as a kind of dress-uniform, a cloak like a lacy shawl, but veined, so that it resembled bees' wings. I badly wanted a picture of the face of his daughter, but all the women of the cult wore veils that made them look like Japanese brides, white swathings tacked to white broad-brimmed hats. It was the ceremonial headgear of a female beemaster, and Madame at that time was one of several bee-initiates; she and her companions formed a 'sisterhood' of identical veiled shapes. A remarkable and compelling appearance like a ghost, but quite simply evolved from the practical working-dress of a beekeeper.

Sudden and extraordinary wealth compensated, it appeared, for the daughter's bereavement, though when the will was published it was clear that her father had left her nothing but the buildings of the then Institute, a largish and fairly run-down house standing in its own grounds on the outskirts of London. With the mysterious influx of money, Jacqueline Petula Dimitrios had bought the Cornish peninsula on which the present Institute now stood, converting to this purpose the indigenous manor-house. The purchase also included a small village complete with church, bank and school; a quarry of useful building-stone;

*See *The Beekeepers* by Peter Redgrove (Stride, 2006).

a repair docks which was a going concern; an ancient harbour of stone-built piers which protected the village's fleet of three fishing vessels; a couple of prosperous farms with arable and grazing-land; and a reclamation project which was draining part of the estuary to convert it into watermeadows. The community was self-contained and self-supporting. The only roads were private ones, closed to the public, and notices warned tourists off by land and sea. Holiday-makers thought of it vaguely as some Ministry of Defence installation or research establishment. Indeed, I was beginning to feel, it was such: the trade of 'facilitator' was a ministry of search and re-search; and it was a ministry that must be protected from the profane. Who were the profane? Those who defamed the 'enthusiastic imagination'.

Among the cuttings was a long article by an investigative journalist who had managed to get taken on as a patient. She reported favourably, and though she commented a good deal on the opulence of the furnishings and appointments, something I had not noticed myself, she described the Institute much as I had found it. There was no use of the word 'facilitator' in the article, and it seemed to me that she did not understand the nature of the treatment, though at least she did not defame it. She said that she was pleased that there was very little religious atmosphere for those who didn't want it. Though Madame kept her own hive-observances and bee-meditations with a small inner group, there was no attempt to proselytise other inmates, as she called them. There was one thing she said that made my head swim, and though it is usually the first matter that one considers, I realised that it had never crossed my mind. She said it was wonderful that there were no fees. Cases were selected on their merit, and no one was impoverished by the treatment, so that they would have the best chance of slipping back into their lives again without crippling debts, and perhaps with a bit saved, as their cost of living was supplied while they were patients. With my other amnesias, I had forgotten all about fees!

Then there was a sudden flood of big black headlines. AMAZING AND MYSTERIOUS DISAPPEARANCE OF BEE-PROPHETESS was their theme, in as many varieties as there were journals. It seemed that a famous West German composer had become interested in the Bee-cult, its rituals and legends. He wished to compose a Mass that was simultaneously a musical composition and a spiritual experiment. It would utilise the bee-hum, already used as a mantra or prayer, and by his musical skill he would make it a triumphant affirmation of their earthy and harmonious religion. The cult would gain fame and new members; members would gain new insight from the musical prayer; art and religion would walk hand in hand. The press latched on to this as though it were a new idea, and as if Mozart, Bach, Beethoven and the innumerable composers who had written religious music had never existed. *The Mass of the Infinite Hive* would be performed privately as a religious service but there would be recordings cut for sale and broadcast. The work was scored for solo cantor and congregation, and rehearsals were carried out behind closed doors and with the utmost secrecy. Inevitably, Madame Dimitrios was billed as soloist.

The arrival of all the initiates past and present at the Institute made a glittering occasion, but television reporting was confined to the lobby. Madame, veiled in golden mesh and dressed with great splendour, was seen sweeping into the hall; a glimpse was obtained of the congregation settling itself; then the great doors closed.

When they opened again two hours later, it was plain that the congregation was moved. Many were crying, but none would speak to the reporters. The media were not worried by this, as Madame had promised an interview. But Madame was nowhere to be found.

Immediately a rumour went round that she had disappeared entirely, had absented herself from her duties at the Institute, had eloped with the West German, or secretly joined an enclosed order of nuns in revulsion from the opulent splendours of her golden religion. Gilded it was; activated by fury at Dimitrios having broken her word to them, the press dug a little further and turned up a gold mine. Jacqueline Dimitrios was revealed to be one of the richest women in the world, having inherited from an American millionaire. It sold copies and gained viewers to wonder at length in print and on the small screen whether Madame Dimitrios was the American's natural daughter or had merely been his physician, and the benefactor a grateful patient. The source of income that paid everybody's fees was now plain, and the poor loonies were not living off the profits of the innocent farmers and fishermen of the peninsula. It was a tremendous scoop for independent television when Jacqueline Dimitrios agreed to appear on their network to demonstrate that she was still alive and active, and that there was no enormous inheritance going begging, or transferred by marriage to West Germany. At this point the cuttings ended, and the book said in large black letters 'Please apply to librarian for telerecording.'

I duly applied, and the librarian helpfully seated me in the viewing cubicle and fitted the spool into the video-recorder. I could hardly control my excitement — at last I was going to see Madame. There were introductory flickers and graphics, and I heard the voice I remembered so well from the relaxation tape remarking 'The reports of my disappearance have been much exaggerated' as I stared at the screen. There was no face. Only a broad-brimmed beekeeper's hat covered with a white veil, the image of disappearance itself.

Disappointed, I returned the spool. As I handed it across the counter, I heard the noise of a printing press, and saw through a half-opened door the red-headed dwarf in an ink-stained apron perched on the stool of a linotype, working busily. My annoyance at being unable to see the face of the woman I intended to marry made me think of how easy it would be to forge newspaper cuttings with the equipment used to print the Institute magazine. After all, how did I know I was not paying fees? Nobody had mentioned the subject to me. One usually received the bill at the end of a stay. By then I would be rich enough by marriage to pay it. So there was no need to think about it at all, ever.

* * * * *

'Or you could have the jacuzzi.' Daniel pointed to the immense sunken tub with the oblique-angled jets built into the rim. He spun one of a complicated series of faucets set into a kind of water-switchboard that resembled the control-console of a hydro-electric power station. The jacuzzi turned to milk as the high-pressure jets began to revolve the body of water in the tub round and round, slowly at first, like a great flywheel.

'But I think with your skin problem you should have either the

Spanish Cloak or the Clay Shirt. Maybe wet sock treatment. All these are standard compresses.'

I slipped my towelling robe off and tried to look backwards at the florid eruption of pimples that I knew covered my shoulder blades. Fresh-faced little Daniel stood behind me, looking upwards at my carbuncled back with all the pleasure of a small boy in a sweet-shop at Christmas.

'Oh, it's the Clay Shirt for you.' He took two woollen blankets from a cupboard and laid them on one of the folding beds in the white-tiled, windowless basement room. We were alone except for the woman I had concluded was a nurse, as she had been helping Xavier with his meal at the special table. I wanted to look at her, for she was small, dark and pretty, but she was also topless. A strong balsamic smell drifted across from where she was sitting in a long calico skirt on one of the small stools with the perforated seats that were standing around. There was a cord snaking away from under her skirt to an electric point. As I watched out of the corner of my eye, her eyes rolled up and she gave a great sigh, wriggling and settling on her seat. A puff of vapour escaped from the folds of her tent-like skirt. There must be some electric kettle or pot charged with a vapourising medicament under her. For a moment I expected her to give forth an utterance in verse like the Sibyl on her tripod, but she merely closed her eyes and seemed to go to sleep. I transferred my attention to the great jacuzzi, rolling in its socket like the eye of a hurricane.

Daniel was now spreading a sheet over the blankets he had smoothed onto the folding bed. Then he went over to a taller cupboard, and as he opened it, I saw hanging inside a row of long white linen shirts like nightgowns. He took one out. I hitched the robe off my shoulders and let it fall.

'Not yet,' said Daniel. There was a large copper pot on a shelf with a ladle resting in it. He took the ladle in his delicate little hand and stirred it round, peering into the pot, inspecting the contents. I saw that this was a pale, smooth mud of clay. Satisfied, Daniel put the shirt into the pot, and pushed it down into the mud with the ladle, stirring it round and round. After doing this thoroughly, he pulled the repulsive garment out with a wooden pincers. It was grey and sopping. He took it by the shoulders and walked across the room to me with it held wide open. I felt that he had disembowelled a corpse and was inviting me to dress in the carcass. He made me put my arms into the heavy dripping sleeves, which were so long they came down over my knuckles, and wrapped me round in the clinging folds, tying them up my front in a neat series of bows with the tapes that were sewn there instead of buttons. He pushed me over to the bed and made me lie down on it, wrapping me first in the sheet, then in the blankets. The clammy chill of the mud-soaked shirt, which at first made me gasp and wrap my arms round myself (and this made it worse since it brought the chill clay closer in contact with my skin), was now becoming replaced with an exceedingly pleasant and gradual warmth, which reached right into my muscles. The cold had brought the blood to my skin, and now the clay, an insulator, was reflecting my own warmth back deep into my body, which made it glow.

I relaxed, and listened to the jacuzzi gently hiss and bubble in its swirl. The sound reminded me of the Bronze Facilitator. As I drifted off to sleep, I heard words begin behind the water-sough, as though some spirit of hydropathics were singing in the Jacuzzi. What message was there for me here? More about ghosts? My credibility played with the idea that in this Institute water was ready to speak whenever it touched metal, that the very pipes in the walls were singing mystery and wisdom all day.

Yet my rational side knew that it was the girl taking her Lower Body Vapour Bath who was singing. My half-dreaming reverie was soothed by the song; it took me deeper; I thought that relaxation, soothing, was sooth, and she was a soothsayer, and that tribute of myrrh and frankincense or other costly unguent was ascending into her lower kingdom, and that these balsamic rubefacients were making the blood sing there, and I was hearing this nether song magnified and detected, as a radio set tunes, detects and demodulates, amplifies the everywhere rippling of the electromagnetic atmosphere. I listened to the song, and descended into it, into its centre, returned to its outskirts, in a rhythmic diastole, systole like the bloods of my heart, like the rhythm of the swirl of water in the great jacuzzi at my side.

This is the Key of the Kingdom:
In that Kingdom is a city;

In that city is a town;
In that town there is a street;
In that street there winds a lane;
In that lane there is a yard;
In that yard there is a house;
In that house there waits a room;
In that room an empty bed;
And on that bed a basket —
A Basket of Sweet Flowers:

Of Flowers, of Flowers;
A Basket of Sweet Flowers.

Flowers in a Basket;
Basket on the bed;
Bed in the chamber;
Chamber in the house;
House in the weedy yard;
Yard in the winding lane;
Lane in the broad street;
Street in the high town;
Town in the city;
City in the Kingdom —
This is the Key of the Kingdom.

Of the Kingdom this is the Key.

Then she was like a Sibyl, on her stool. The ghost of certain people older than their years might speak out so in an ancient song, a nursery song — how else was wisdom to be passed down except in the openness of the trance-state of childhood? My young lullaby-singing lunatic (if otherwise, why should she be here?) had found the song revolving still somewhere at her centre, where her sooth relaxation found it; and she was causing all the pockets, fistulas, blind alleys and caverns of her balsamic body to vibrate or rematerialise this song, giving it a new body of air to speak with. Was that willed resurrection of a helpful impulse or spirit the Kingdom itself? Or was the Kingdom the manner in which the song's soothsaying was clearing the clouds of my mind so that I could perceive, but still calmly, the whirlpool of my fearful psyche swirling and spitting just under the appearance of things. I seemed to be offered many memories that were not my own. I had a sudden vision that was like people crammed in a brightly lit tunnel in some obscene and immortal rush-hour, jostling together for so long that their beards and hair had grown white, and billowed over them like a plasm; and the coiling hair was crammed with eyes turning every way.

* * * * *

I do not know what happens to her when she enters that church. I see her dip her fingers in the holy water and cross herself but it is more like a caress. I have seen her hug herself after bringing herself off. She dresses in this suit and this frilly blouse and she goes to see God as one might go to the public library and change a book. Yet it is the same book; a nasty fat piece of work in leather that splits open on creamy-white pages full of big letters that buzz like bluebottles. Like bluebottles they cluster around the subjects of death, graveyards, piles of foreskins, dying by torture, hell. As if there were nothing else worth reading, it is called in Latin *The Book,* and subtitled *The Jesus Murder.*

Yes, there is a smell about her going to that church. It is masochistic lechery. The grey suit, that looks so slippery and stifling, filled with her softness that foams out of the openings like water whitened by a weir, like a spate over a clay bed. And that simper which tells me she is off to see God.

It is principally in church that my thoughts wander. It may be that they are running away very hard from God. Or towards him. God and his virgins. God the successful, who controls the thought-police. And my girl who wanders off to God dressed in a maddening suit and frills. She comes home and she strips the jacket off and I need to screw her among those water-and-foam ruffles, and I do so; but I think God got there first. I was going to talk about God. He has made me jealous. They say he is a jealous God — let him command me, let him command my obedience — I will do anything, so that he commands it. But that is not how it works out. It is I who am jealous, and obedient.

I am jealous of her, and of all the people whom he makes think of him, incessantly. I am sitting now in this nice cool church with the grey stone pillars and the fragrant dust and the coloured windows of peaceable men in long robes and beards. One of them comes to see me in my pew.

'Excuse me, can I help at all?'

'What do you mean? Am I not entitled to sit here? It is hot outside.'

'That is not what I mean. You are disturbing the other worshippers.'

'There is nobody else here except you.'

'You are disturbing the air. Others may have decided not to enter because of the shouting inside the church.'

'What was this shouting?'

'God, God, God, said several times rapidly.'

'Entirely suitable in a church.'

'The times of public worship are posted.'

'Look here, Vicar, this man who was shouting, I daresay he was in great distress of mind.'

'Would you like to speak to the Vicar? I am the sacristan, Stanley.'

'Where is he?'

'At the moment he is at the psychiatrist. He will be free soon.'

'I hope so. What's the trouble?

'I don't see that it's any business of yours, Mister Ah.'

'What the Vicar does at the psychiatrist is the business of all God-fearing people, I should think.'

'He is there for nail-biting. It got so bad that his finger-ends would spout blood when he was praying.'

'I should say that is repressed masturbation.'

'Are you a psychiatrist or doctor?'

'I am a traveller. One may deepen one's prayer by masturbating.'

'He was leaving terrible bloody handprints all over the church and in the big pulpit Bible. You may see them in the big Bible supported on the lectern's eagle wings, if you turn to Numbers and Deuteronomy.'

'I will certainly consider looking them up.'

'He wore white cotton gloves but they were soon sopping. Like one of those dreadful Italian Easter miracles.'

'What will you do if I continue to cry out on God in your church?'

'I will call for the police.'

'Who will cry out for the psychiatrist. I want to see the Vicar.'

'You will have to wait until the psychiatrist has finished with him.'

'Then I must wait quietly.'

'God Bless you, sir.'

'God Bless you quietly.'

And he wandered away. I needed men like that to tell me what I was doing, after I had crossed the line which marked the place where I ceased to know I was doing it, imperceptible threshold. And whether my behaviour was acceptable when I had got to that invisible, empty place. I want to cross that threshold conscious. This is why I am jealous of God, so full, so full of Vicars and women telling him who he is, reciting his qualities, so that he need never lose himself anywhere in his plenum. I have an empty space in me, ready for God to inhabit, but he stays away. I might decorate it with cries, I might hang it with flowers and love, I might soothe it with sex, or fire guns into it to start God like a hare running, but there's only me there, I think.

Loud cries came out of that emptiness without my knowledge or connivance. I would wait outside for the woman to come clip-clopping in high heels over the grave paving inscribed with flowers and cherubs. I love this emblem of the hand reaching down from the cloud and clasping the dead man's hand that reaches up out of his soil. You see it on many stones in this boneyard. There is the cuff of a shroud, and the cuff is frilly, as if fizzing up its sleeve with excitement at God's touch. God's hand is naked.

Here is a curious one. *Donald Holliday. 1935-1981.* That puts his ghost into its mid-forties. But there's a metal mirror nailed to the stone. And a legend. 'Regard this glass; as you are, I once was.' Damn cheek. I can see nothing but black spreading trees of tarnish in this mirror. Ugh! The ground stuffed with empty shells, ageing disastrously, having given up their ghosts. And to put a mirror on one's gravestone, as if the ghost were still gliding within, watcher from its casement. Hole-in-the-Day. Holiday.

What is the age of the ghost of our marriage? We used to call it 'passing the ghost' when she came. I felt the shudder of the feathery thing passing over her body. The frilled collar and cuffs were the sign of the presence of this thing, as the little red light of the oil lamp hanging over the small iron door above the little piscina signals the presence of God's red ghost, older than the earth. Her cup runneth over. Ah, a little shower is passing overhead.

Oh, I hope she comes now, while it is still raining, comes hurrying, under the soft ghost of the rain passing into the puddles, trampling them, the grey suit a little blackened with drops soaking into her shoulders, as if the ghost had soft fangs, and were drinking her. She would dart inside daintily, frills panting like gills. Rain frightens her, but it gives me a beautiful tingling stand! I would give anything to have her in the rain, in that rainy, frilly blouse. But I'd have to be God to get that. How old is the rain's ghost?

She finds in her loins a hole in the day for God to enter. She once called out 'God, my God,' when the ghost was passing between us, and we were shivering for love, and the hair was starting up along my spine, like wind in a wheatfield. Then she opened her eyes and looked at me and smiled very sweetly and the whole atmosphere changed, as when a thundery rain falls. 'God, my God,' she said again very softly, looking at me. We were young, of course. I swear I have tried to live up to her opinion of me at that instant. I have tried to find God within, but there is only this empty space, unconscious, and of immeasurable age.

Where was God, that she could find him in this ancient, empty building, this hole built of rock? His people point to that hanging red light above the locked cupboard, singing 'Of the Kingdom this is the Key'. I took the bread and wine once, without preparation, without confession, just to see what it was like, and that was a mortal sin, and I felt the feathering dry touch of it, and tasted the sharp wine, and I felt Sin travelling through all my pipes, and I wanted to invite him in to lodge in me and grow, but I suppose he came out in the ordinary way, and travelled on. As I shall do when I enter the food-chain, from grave-weed to honey-hive to the soft lips of her munching her elementary bread-and-honey. Shall that pollen and sugar stay in her and germinate into a child? Bah! it is a fantasy. I felt that the food of God might lodge in certain women, and, as we spread butter on bread, spread wide their legs when they came home from church, and lay them humbly fertile on the hall carpet. It might well be to God's purpose to take them then and there, before they got their church clothes off.

Here she comes! Yes, a little speckled with the shower, smelling of daffodils from her talc. I slip into the church after her. She crosses herself with holy water, and bobs to the font. To the font! It should be the altar. I can get at her from here. Let me try a hollow voice, vaulting to the ceiling.

'Cecilia!'

'What?'

'It is God, Cecilia, speaking from the water.'

'Oh, it's you. You made me jump. You mustn't play about like that here. Where are you, I can't see you.'

'It is God, at last, Cecilia, speaking to you. I want to see you tonight, among the tombs, in that big puddle by Donald Holliday's grave, Cecilia, and don't bother to change your clothes.'

'Oh you! You're very disrespectful.'

'To you, or God?' I asked, stepping out from behind my pillar.

'To God, of course.'

'Come now, do you think he minds banter and a little bit of the other between wedded people who are a mystery to each other?'

'Church is for a different kind of feeling.'

'Groans and howls.'

'I like to worship here, by myself, in God's way.'

'Are you going to punish me for coming to the Church and ambushing your bush?'

'God will punish you.'

'He already has.'

'Oh, very fine. How?'

'By emptying me.'

'You talk enough about it.'

'Empty vessels. Am I mad, Cecilia?'

'You are irresponsible.'

'I was groaning for God in here.'

'I tell you it's the proper place for it.'

'Without knowing I was.'

'That shows an instinct for the Source.'

'It can't be the same as yours, goose. I want to talk to you about a gander God we can share, whatever the gender.'

'And then you want a fuck.'

'Cecilia, it's the same thing. We come to a point when words will no longer do.'

'Can't you rest in faith?'

'No, my restlessness which is my sex, renews hourly. Hollow-daily.'

'The worm that dieth not.'

'You meet God here like a secret lover, wriggling through the apple. And I am jealous.'

'Are you? Well, he's a greater lover than you are.'

'"God wrought her with his hand all naked." I know. Therefore he's a fuck, or it's an echo of him. He made us to fuck, passing ghosts between us, calling us out of nothing to worship him. We have the memory of union with him when our souls were created in a woman; we seek to return there, your holiness.'

Out of the corner of my eye I saw the sacristan coming towards me. No doubt I had been bellowing again. Yes, there was a policeman just entering the double doors. He had stopped there, faced with the ticklish problem of whether to take his uniform helmet off in a place of God when he was there on official business. The Vatican had a better scheme, with its own police. I did not want to strike the sacristan Stanley, or maim him. I was capable of it. A man of sixty is in the prime of life so far as I am concerned, if his ghost is young. I thought I would merely detain him. I scooped a pile of hymnbooks off the little shelf that was overwhelmed and tilted with them. I thrusted them in his arms. I lifted another pile. He was overflowing with hymnbooks now and could only grab me by impiously dropping them. I gave him another load and walked rapidly down the further aisle towards the vestry. I swung the big solid door shut, and bolted it behind me. That would keep them out! I saw white surplices and black gowns hanging on a rail, peeping from behind heavy purple curtains like a crowd of headless people. There were dusty hassocks strewn about in the space below them. They looked so comfortable I thought I would sit on one and give my heart a rest. It was pounding so hard in my vaulted chest it reminded me of a man bellowing about God in church. As I wriggled back further among the hassocks the smell of beeswax and the old wood was so pleasant and restful I thought I'd lie down for a brief spell. I pulled a surplice like a sheet down on top of me. The cloth with its gatherings was harsher than I imagined. The people had stopped pounding on the vestry door into the church. I heard a rattle and a clink, and a shaft of sunlight fell into my hiding place as the other vestry door to the graveyard opened. I drew my legs in so the sun should not touch them.

* * * * *

The psychiatrist was a flapper half my age.

'How long have you been sixty?' I boggled at her question.

'Long enough to acquire two wives, several close companions, two books of poetry written, a few friends, a teen-age son who looks exactly like me, a PhD in rocket engineering, a long list of my dead, and the face you see me with.'

'It was your birthday I wanted.'

'January. They say Capricorns are old goats, and take a long time to start anything. Once started, they are unstoppable. That's what they say.'

'Who say?'

'All the nuts who believe in it.'

'Perhaps it's just conversation.'

'I thought conversation was your trade. The talking cure. People behave according to the labels other people stick on to them.'

'Is that why you claim to be sixty?'

'You've got my date of birth there.' I was getting cross with her.

'No, I'm afraid I haven't. Your papers haven't arrived.'

'My papers . . .' This was beginning to sound like the conversations I had with Cecilia, which ended with me bellowing. Come to think of it, this stripling a little resembled Cecilia. Younger, of course. I liked her sleek and shiny blouse, open like a lily at the neck. A little heavy, in folds, and shiny, as if wet. A woman stepping towards me between the gravestones with open full throat in the rain is the apparition or angel of God, the annunciating throat preparing raptures, hovering on the white collar-wings.

'But you look to me like a much younger man.' As she kept returning to the attack, I decided to pretend I was married to her, and she was Cecilia.

'I like to keep in shape.'

'No, younger than that.' Then after a pause, she said,

'If you're as young as you feel, then what age is that?'

'Sixty. I feel mature, though healthy.'

'The police say that at your age you should have learnt how to behave in church.'

'Well, what do you think, Doctor? I am insanely jealous of God. I claim the right to discuss important matters with the King in his Castle.'

'What do I think? I agree with you, of course. You should come to my Institute.'

'Can I afford it?'

'Can you afford not to. There are no fees.'

'What do you get out of it?'

'Experience and . . .' I am a little deaf, and I thought she then said 'lovers' as she turned away to look out of the window, though it must have been 'love'. I was roused by the thought, and determined to find out by going there what she meant. She turned around again, swinging in the wings of her big desk chair.

'If you feel sixty now, what age would you be if you turned black?'

'Black?' The entire point of my secret was its blackness, and its rejuvenation. It abridged the age of my ghost.

'Black, you say? That would be very nice. I would feel young! I would give birth to myself, to my own black son. I would be proud of my black skin, and never abuse it with objects like these.' I began to struggle out of my clothes. I thought then, even as I did it, that the Doctor would react badly, as if we were not married, and that I would probably go to prison. I had not understood the calibre of this physician.

'There,' I said, as I pulled off my string vest and stepped out of my underpants, 'that's much better!' My blackness gleamed in the sunshine through the window. My penis hovered attentively, beaked like a raptor, looked knotty and useful.

'That's better,' she said. The blouse and the black skirt had evaporated; she was not black, I saw to my sorrow; on the contrary, the sun shone on her also, and she seemed covered with a fine golden fur. The whole atmosphere had changed, and she was smiling. 'Afterwards you must come and see by bees.' I spread myself out on the carpet like the wings of my beak. But it was my prey that hovered above me, and stooped like a raptor, and strong arms and a strong cunt gripped me. A tremendous charge shot up my spine. Something unrolled from me, and I fell head-first into energy! I opened my eyes and was blinded with fizzing energy! I took my body in both hands at the front and ripped it off me. I saw my grey skin go swirling by, whitening like a ghost as the hampering clay dissolved. I struggled to my feet and stood up in the jacuzzi. I drew a great breath, and my whole body tingled with it. I waded waist high through the water to the bench below water-level at the edge of the bath and sat down. The whirling, champagne-bubbled, lacy water speeded round my neck; I tucked my chin in and sat with my spine straight and let my beard soak in the water that smelt faintly of pine and which went bubbling forcefully round and round my body as though I were sitting in a stream of spirits at a new kind of seance. I felt inspired; I determined that I would study to set down such feelings as these in poetry; they were too natural and too worthy to be lost; I would write poetry that was like a clay shirt that warmed you unexpectedly and like a jacuzzi that woke your skin. I would find some way of saying this well! The empty shirt swirled round and round in the water, dabbing me with its empty sleeves. I fished for it and chucked it with a slap on the stone sill of the bath. It was dazzlingly white, even though it was sopping. Daniel came in and looked at me smiling.

'You have found your way into the jacuzzi, I see. But do you remember how you got there?'

'Yes,' I replied. I would fill my pen with a certain ink. The young Sibyl dozed on her perforated seat.

* * * * *

I came upon Sir Geoffrey sorting a big pile of dry paper pages, crisp as autumn leaves.

'May I look through these?'
'Of course.'
There was a fair one about Madame as a feral courtesan. I grew jealous as I read it, and looked sideways at Sir Geoffrey. Was this loony really a contender?

FUR, NOT FURY

Madame is fur-sheathed,
Marmalade-furred
From the roots of the breasts
To the back of the toes,

Coppery leotard,
Dark striping the gold,
Colour of Venus. As I stared,
Smiling she said:

'No part of me is dangerous;
There are certain advantages;
Come to bed.'
And there were

In the skin of catspaw
That moiré'd with feelings;
Her fur stood on end
Like a bed of soft thorns, that yielded then

In moth-beats like a rain of feathers.
What in most is kept
Cunt-closed, in her
Was pelt, and palpable bee-burr;

And later I asked her
'Nurture or nature?'
'As in a field of wheat
That ripples as the spirit listeth,

'I lay in my skin;
When my body furred
I refused to be feared;
Stay with me, let your skin

'Reach out to me.
Not fury, fur.
Fur, not fear.'

Bees not fees! I much preferred the one about Madame Dimitrios's Smile. It was a golden smile, and it betrayed her feelings. If it were a traitor, might it not also be a liar? What of it, I thought; it was worth it, that smile.

She tells me the polished skull of a traitor
Lurks in this well still,
His comrades gave rough justice,
Over the parapet laid his bare neck,
Cutlass-sliced that smuggling head,
Which dropped like a boulder
And is down there to this day, she said,

Polished nearly to nothing,
Bobbing in the well-spring,
Folding and unfolding in the polishing water,
Almost glass, and papery-thin,
Ascending, descending on variable cool water,
Nodding upon a current which is a spine,
Spinning like a film of faintest shadow
Or flexible churchwindow,
Reflating when rain fattens the spring;
Then a sunbeam
Strikes down the brick shaft
And there gazes upwards, revolving in the depths,
A golden face; then the sun

Goes in and the water goes on polishing.

* * * * *

'Let me help you with your veil.'

The tall black beekeeper known as Sir Geoffrey solicitously adjusted the crown of the hat I was wearing, to the brim of which were tacked swathes of coarse muslin. I tried to keep my mind off the fact that he was stark naked.

'It's OK,' I said, 'just these stray long bits.'

'Tuck them in your shirt collar. You want to be careful. Bees can be fierce.'

I glanced at his naked form. 'That doesn't seem to bother you much.'

'No,' he said, 'they're used to me. I smell like bees, I expect.'

'I came by the gym on the way to see you. I thought the bees were loose. It was humming like an angry hive.'

'Oh, that was Daniel. He's very good at the humming. But he never comes here in case he gets stung.'

'He doesn't look the nervous type.'

'He's not. But if he does get stung he swells terribly. They have to get a special doctor in. He swells so fast that his own face is likely to suffocate him if nothing is done. It may surprise you to know that hypnotism works, antihistamines not.'

'I have a great respect for hypnotism. I find the bee-hum hypnotic.'

'Well, it is. We have learnt to prize it. Why not go to one of Daniel's training-sessions? Humming perks you up like nothing else I know.'

'It refreshes parts other sounds cannot reach.'

'It is OM. You had better wear gloves.'

'What was the name of the man who laid his hand on the side of the Ark of the Lord, and the Lord struck him down?'

'They're quite safe if I use my "puffer". The smoke of the burning wood relaxes them. The tops lift off so, like the lids of packing-cases. Now you can see the racks, oozing with honey and dripping with bees, each one humming like a saint!'

'So many! Like a shining black liquid that sings. Thousands and thousands, dangling in bunches like grapes. Is it safe?'

'Quite safe in the veil. Nothing can get in, or out. Though these days their food is the flowers, which feed on the sun; once, long ago, before they evolved, bees were meat-eaters. Their ancestors were wasps. Then, they would have stripped you and torn your heart out, piranhas of the air.'

'My heart, humming like a red hive.'

'You really must do those exercises.'

'I've seen wasps flying away with bits of bloody sawdust picked off the butcher's floor.'

'Everything came from the work of bees. They pollinated the flowers which grew into the forests. Our ancestors came from the trees. I would like to show you some of my poems.'

'When do you write?'

'In the night-time.'

'This humming is the sound of satisfaction, AH UM — like a good stretch.'

'You have it. The hum facilitates, like nothing else. Or so Madame's father used to say. His first advice to anybody was "Think of bees." He started these hives. Madame says that bees are too fiery for beginners, and advises them to listen to the sound of water in Aristotle's head instead. These hives are powerhouses on stilts. Yet they are gentle to those they know.'

'I was fascinated as a child by a photo I saw in *Titbits* of an American who fascinated bees so that they swarmed over his face like a beard. Then he would take a shower wearing his beard-bees.'

'That is advanced teaching!' Sir Geoffrey spoke harshly, 'too advanced for anybody who wants to stay human, in my opinion. Yet it began well. *Fit sonitus, mussantque oras et limina circum*: "What a harmony you hear as they murmur around their policies and thresholds." There is harmony everywhere in the air and in the earth, and the bees make it manifest. You can hear it in the hum full of stings; you can see it in the strict cities of hexagonal wax; harmony is sweet, and you can taste it in the honey and comb. David Dimitrios taught his initiates to touch and feel it too, by plunging their bodies in the hives so that the bees would run over their entire skin. If you flinched, you were unfit, and likely to be stung to death. If you endured their multifarious touch, then, it is said, it gave you transports of ecstasy. But his bee-men — they reverted. At the end they were wasps!'

Sir Geoffrey dwarfed me. I looked up at his black face. I thought he meant WASPs, and racial prejudice. There were tears in his eyes, and as I watched a bee landed on the corner of his eyelid and began drinking from the spring there.

'Is that why you wear no clothes?'

'Do you not care for my colour?' I was right; he was angry.

'I'm sorry. There's a lot I have to learn. What happened to Madame's father?'

'He was blown to pieces.'

'Sorry again.'

'Do you know what I was when I came to this Institute?'

'No.'

'I was white. This is an improvement, is it not?'

'Yes, Sir Geoffrey.'

'I prefer to stay unclothed in order to emphasise this.'

'Of course.'

'I'd like to show you one of my poems now.'

He ducked into his dusty beekeeper's hut. I saw through the door a line of the Japanese-looking veil-hats hanging on pegs. There were eight, four with black muslin, four with white. Sir Geoffrey emerged with a big scrolled paper covered with odd black writing, fuzzy as the bodies of bees, and handed it to me. I watched him slide the living combs back into their racks, and close the top of the hive by replacing the lid. I noticed five or six bees wandering over his gleaming shoulder blades and up and down his spine. I shivered, and read. It was a poem I felt I knew well.

* * * * *

('The top of the dressing-table was littered with the usual teenager rubbish of spilt powder, chipped pocket-mirrors, eyebrow-brushes, little boxes of cosmetic paint. At the left hand, a tall candle in a pewter holder. Jackie puts on tall eyebrows with a black pencil; this detail gives her a supercilious Japanese look. The mirror-light comes from a fluorescent strip, drowning the candle. Jackie finishes. She bares her teeth in the mirror, tries on in quick succession a simper, an angry smile, a frown, an impassive Japanese expression. She decides to maintain this last for her evening's face. She snaps out the strip-lighting, and makes a curious slow fanning gesture in front of the candle. Like this.'

Madame spreads the fingers of her left hand, which she shakes to and fro slowly in front of her veil. We have been invited to another seance, but there is no materialisation cabinet up, and she is sitting with us in a circle of ordinary armchairs. She is telling us a story, and I am rather glad of this, as the last seance I found rather fierce. She has explained to us that we should all try to find our way of making a 'hole in the day'. For some it is a seance; for others a special kind of bath, in the relaxation of which ordinary time stops; it may be a special trade, like beekeeping, in which one becomes absorbed; it may be a story told, in which the space and timing of the story's figures take over our own, and we must try to remember if we knew it, how bedtime stories were, when we relaxed and listened as children. All were 'holes in the day' that let some other world in.

'Jackie's room has a wall-to-wall carpet, creamy in colour. There is a small brass bed with a white coverlet. On the wall beside it is a poster of a singer with spiky orange hair, a letterbox mouth, and a microphone like a black toffee-apple. Jackie stares thoughtfully at this poster of a possessed singer. There are a number of smaller pictures fastened to the walls of this room: contorted singers. One photograph shows a black woman in a white dress kneeling and howling, the throat exposed and swollen, and gripped in her right hand a large darkly marked snake escaping off the edge of the picture. Jackie turns back to the dressing-table and sweeps a number of items off it into her handbag. She catches sight of the orange-haired singer in her mirror, turns, crosses to her bed and rips the poster off the wall. It leaves an unsightly blotch on the white where the glue has plucked the distemper away. Jackie scrunches it in her free hand. The spare room is a few steps along the corridor. On her way downstairs, she throws the screwed-up poster on to its uncarpeted floor.' I relaxed, and Madame's voice turned into scenes.)

Jackie's Grannie is making slow and painful progress upstairs, sliding the arthritic claw which is her left hand up the banister. She smiles at Jackie.

'If it isn't our Cinderella. Off to the Disco again. Watch the clock for midnight, or you'll be dancing in tatters, Cindy.'

Grannie's coiffure is an immense steely-blue concoction, emphatic as the prow of an old ship. It rises and descends in rigid billows, with the curious effect of imparting as much detail to the back of her head as exists on the front, where her face is.

Thus, when she lowers her eyes to take care that her feet have not missed the stair, for she is old, there seems to be a great mask of hair facing backwards that rears up. It is like a figure-head to her dignified and ample stern.

'Oh, have you bought my pumpkin for tonight, fairy Godmother? Look to it; I want dapple grey mice in the reins; and there are radishes in the kitchen who will make beautiful rosy footmen. I shall wear tonight the dress like starlight in my great series of wonder-awakening dresses. How's the hand, Grannie?'

'Same as always, dear. Doesn't like the wet weather much.'

'I'll say it a prayer at the dance.'

'You do that, dear.'

(Was a hole in the day to let the night in? Were dreams holes in the night? Yeats kept a hole in the day open by means of Swedish exercises and ritual magic; light streamed through this hole and illuminated his nights: all his dreams were brightly sunlit. Madame was disingenuous in not making a complete list, surely. A hole is a hole; intercourse and masturbation should have been included, royal roads.)

The Disco was hot, noisy and small. It swirls, like a jacuzzi, its circular motion imparted to the inmates by means of the whirling disc on the turntable, and in its air, heavy as water, the faces float like bubbles and the dresses like currents. Some dancers pound on the spot, the men with rotating suggestive gestures of their hips and amazed gesticulations of the upper limbs; the women with clenched fists miming aggressive acceptance of these thrusts, slightly out of sync, so that the dance shall not seem totally explicit. The faces express themselves independently of the bodies; in light conversation or the Elvis-sneer of boredom. Some bodies have gripped each other in the old-fashioned style, and glidingly circulate, those inconvenient faces turned away.

Jackie wishes to dance solo, as she has a spell to make. Her Kabuki face with its impassivity contrasts with her fast and energetic movements: she shakes it (in the old parlance) and she shakes it like a twenties barman mixing a Harvey Wallbanger. She began dancing near the centre of the floor, but she has been elbowed by the couples occupying, as it were, the eye of the storm, into the outskirts, where the bodies are closely united and circulate more freely, and from thence to her own space by a white wall, flowing with oily colours from the revolving and flashing strobe lights. In her light dress and white face she becomes those colours, soaked in them like moving camouflage. She will do two hundred steps of this dance, beginning with her Grannie's hand screwed into a claw as it is, and counting backwards; and as the numbers become smaller and simpler, so the hand will ease and unknot into simpler movements so at last at one it will be whole and single. She knows that when she does such things, there is a particular suspended feeling, as though she had entered and passed through some surface. The way she has of doing this is to fan her hands across a light, preferably a flickering one, like a candle. The strobe is a super-flicker, and she has manoeuvred herself to face the lights that are producing this paisley flow all over her as though she were a tattooed Maori. As she spreads her fingers wide and fans them in front of her eyes, their flicker in the light like watered silk produces a strange moiré effect, as when wave sources interrupt, or as when you fold a muslin veil and pass the two surfaces the one across the other, looking out.

(Madame illustrated again the fanning, with her fingers spread, and she took a fold of her veil and lifted it up against the light from the standard-lamp, to show the moiré of the folds crossing each other. An interaction, I thought, which must be continuous to one looking out from the swathes of this veil.)

Without warning beyond the moiré the dancers slowed in their various rotations and stopped quite still. The sound of the music slid deeper and deeper down the scale until it was a bass humming. The dancers were frozen in their attitudes, and to Jackie's horrified eyes began to decay; the coloured lights had fallen now unmoving on their flesh and clothes, and seemed to eat them away like acid resting on cloth or skin. Wounds grew in the faces, across the foreheads, down the cheeks, dissolving lips and enlarging mouths into letter-box holes that grinned, flesh and clothing hung in tatters. The bass hum was still descending in pitch, it was vibrating the floor, and Jackie knew that when it stopped, passed out of audibility's limit, then the dry bones would drop to the floor, and powder, and blow away, and the world would be gone.

She had counted 106 steps of her dance, unwinding her Grannie's hand. She must forget that; it could not be cured at this cost, by this means. She must wind her dance up again, counting forward to the place where it began, reversing her steps. As she did so, the wounds healed, the clothes stitched themselves together again, and at two hundred, with the lights and the music flowing at their normal speed, Jackie fell forward on her unemotional Japanese face with a crash that stopped the music, now going happily forwards, unaware of having almost reached its null point, beyond which was the unpicking of its fabric.

Jackie's friends had been watching her dance. Now they rushed on to the floor and supported her back to their table, watched by the whole room. Then the DJ got his machine in its groove again, and interest faded from the faces and descended into the dancing bodies, as one sees at night a lighted elevator descending storeys.

(Then there are drugs, including tobacco and alcohol. And, as we have just heard, dancing. I wonder whether this is Madame? I have doubts, after all that has happened, though she has the voice of the tapes, and that smile radiates behind the veil. I wish I could see the face! The voice and the smile — well, air-hostesses learn such skills, become one standard air-hostess.)

'She always flakes out when we go dancing.' This is incorrect. It is Lena herself who gets the dramatic headaches.

'She's a lovely dancer . . .' Sue thinks so, being fat and clumsy. 'A lovely dancer . . . it seems to, well, transport her . . .'

Bob, Lena's friend, for whom she edits herself into sweetness, guffaws.

'Transport caff . . .' is his witticism.

Sue snaps at this: 'You just want us all to be scrubbers and slags.'

Jake has been kissing Jackie gently; he is Jackie's real friend; they are not yet quite close; this is an opportunity for him to show care.

Sue is gooseberry to the quartet; to make up for this she must go on talking.

'Jackie can tell fortunes and cast spells when she's been dancing.' Lena snorts. This makes matters much worse. 'It's true, it's true,' says Sue. Jackie is sitting up now and looking round her. She smiles at Sue.

'Tell my fortune then, Jackie, tell mine,' mocks Lena, and

Bob's leer gets broader. He wiggles his hands in front of Jackie's face. 'Come on, Jackie, do the mystic passes.' Jake is disapproving, but does nothing. Jackie's fingers on her lap unconsciously repeat Bob's gesture. She looks down at them, surprised. Lena turns away and whispers in Bob's ear.

Once again Jackie's fingers wriggle and stretch, and she raises them to her face and looks at Lena through them, the white Japanese face with the strongly marked eyebrows and red lips. Lena is equal to this.

'Go on then, Jackie. I bet you can't tell me what I'm thinking.'

'Oh yes I can, Lena.' She turns to Bob. 'It's OK, Bob. No sweat. It's come. You're both quite safe, this time. Lena's got the curse.'

(Madame stopped her story and sipped at her coffee. 'You see how easy it is to become a negative facilitator. What at other times would be called a "witch". A little perception, a little playing on other people's fears.')

Lena gets up hurriedly, spilling assorted objects from her handbag. Jackie pays no attention to her. She is still watching Bob. Again she raises her fingers and fans them in front of her face. One of her hands falters and drops and creeps below the table, plucking at the hem of her skirt. Her Kabuki expression crumples, her eyes grow round and her finger shoots out, pointing rigidly at Bob.

'Oh, he's dead,' she calls out. 'His head rolls and lolls. Bob! watch the wheels . . . oh, it smashes like red flowers . . .'

('I once had a vision,' remarks Xavier, 'of my head crushed. The pressure of the great wheels on the tarmac and their slow rolling had crushed all the fluid matter away. All there was left was a smeared mask of skin overlaid on crushed bones, and a fish-shape like mosaic where the hard teeth were pressed flat into the asphalt.' Madame nods at him, smiles and resumes.)

Jackie is tearing at her neat room. All the photos are down, the white walls scarred. The shiny little brass bed is half-dismantled. Jackie is wheeling one of the two sets of bedrails along the corridor to the spare room.

'What on earth are you up to, Jackie! Don't you realise it's half past one in the morning?'

'I'm working, Father.'

'Work?' He comes upstairs, a stolid and sallow-skinned man with wiry hair and slight jowls, small brilliant eyes in pouches. 'Your room! your nice room!' He stands at the door of it, not knowing what to say. He recollects his mission.

'I'm afraid I've got bad news. The hospital just rang.'

'About Bob?'

'Bob? Yes. How did you know?'

'He's had an accident.'

'Is this one of the things you know?'

'It's just a coincidence, Daddy. They were upset. The roads were slippery with rain. Bob had a hipflask. He was putting something in their drinks. Lena's period had come. They were going off to celebrate.'

'Celebrate? Well, there's nothing to celebrate now. Bob's dead. It was Lena who insisted that they rang here. She was hysterical. Something about a curse. She insisted you be told. I thought it was you when they said it was the hospital. Then I heard that god-awful squeaking upstairs from those castors. Oh hell,' Grannie's door had opened a crack, 'now we've woken up Grandmother. It'll be an all-night milk and biscuit session now. It's all right, Mother. Nothing to worry about. I'll tell you all about it in the morning.'

'I wish you wouldn't call me Mother,' said Grannie sleepily, rubbing her eyes with her claw.

('You'll say that Daddy doesn't sound much like David Dimitrios, I expect,' interposed Madame. 'It's my stepfather. Mother took me away from David. Because of "unnatural practices" she said. My new father was boringly normal.'

'So you had to assert yourself,' said somebody.

'You shall hear,' said Madame. 'The girls at school were boringly normal too. When I heard them muttering about me, it made me proud. They already liked to say that my Grannie was a witch, because she was little and old and had a hideous hair-do instead of a witch's hat and a claw instead of a hand. It stood to reason that I was her apprentice. Plenty of the girls who were good at the conventional things like hockey or lacrosse or golf did obviously magical things, like holes-in-one — but that was called luck. For the loner who was a good guesser, the shy one with the odd Grannie, it was as obviously witchcraft. I played into their hands with the bottle-spinning game, but I couldn't help myself. Nor could Lena, eating her heart out.')

'With five people in the group, chance alone will give us five hits during twenty-five spins. Anything more than that cannot be accounted for by chance, so it must be psychokinesis, witchcraft, or excellent reflexes,' said the studious-looking girl with the big glasses.

'I can see,' says a girl in tennis gear dreamily, 'I can just see those championship bottle-spinning finals on the centre court at Wimbledon.'

'Here comes Jackie. She can do it if anyone can,' says Gig-lamps.

'Yes, she can do it, I expect. If you can see death, you can spin a bottle.' Lena speaks with difficulty. Her mouth is stiff and swollen, her face bruised.

'Look Jackie, it's an ESP game. The operator spins the bottle and must choose one of us as a target. We all concentrate on that person. If when the bottle stops it is pointing at the target-person, then that is a hit. If you get more than five hits in thirty-five spins with seven people here then it's not chance, so the explanation must lie elsewhere. Such as control of the bottle's spinning by the mind's force alone. Which is called psychokinesis and that's what poltergeists do.'

'I'm game,' says Jackie.

'Then choose your target.'

'Whoever it points to first.'

Jackie enters the circle of girls and takes hold of the cloudy-sided milk bottle and spins it on the grey asphalt. As it whirls on its side the bottle makes an insistent grinding noise until it comes to rest pointing directly at Lena, who narrows her eyes and hunches her shoulders and half-turns her back, but does not leave the circle. Jackie takes hold of the bottle again and starts it twirling with a firm twist, then sits back on her haunches. The bottle comes to rest like a small cannon with its glass muzzle pointing directly at Lena. Jackie bends forward and spins again with the impassive face of a roulette gambler or Kabuki witch. It comes to rest pointing directly at Lena, who would, if she had been wise, have left the circle then and there and broken the spell. Instead she feels a hollow in her chest and presses her hand to it, and tries to outstare Jackie's glass instrument of insult; she thought she had been pregnant with Bob, and wished it; this is like some imputation of infertility, the sadness of her imagination of what could have been, taking her out of schoolgirlishness, quickened by the schoolgirls' playground spell; empty breast, empty bottle.

Now Jackie does what superstitious gamblers do with their carved and spotted bones, fondling them and whispering to them before they make their throw. She blows across the top of the bottle making a lowing note and thinks how her fingers in the Disco in their moiré blur seemed to pluck wavering threads through the air, and how her candle did the same in a darkened room, shadows flattened on the walls and ceilings, pulling tufts of darkness through hanks of light, light into darkness and dark into light, jumping the one into and out of the other; and like the Jack-a-dandy of sunbeams on the ceiling from a bowl of water (dip your hand in and he dances, beating his wife with a silver stick) with my breath that speaks moirés through the air and into the minds of others, I quicken life into this creature of glass and say 'catch hold of my enemy's skein, tangle there . . .'; and sings in a whisper:

Point to the one I'm working on,
Jack be Nimble, Jack be Quick,
Bottle like a crystal bone,
Spin your round and take your pick

and spins the bottle, which comes to rest pointing directly at Lena, who is now breathing rapidly with anger and fear. Jackie picks up the bottle. This time when she sings to it all the girls except Lena sing too in a rapid whisper. Lena stands half-cowering like an elected victim at the apex of what had been a circle but which is now an ellipse, with spinner at one culmination and victim entangled at the other. The bottle spins, and points directly at Lena. The chant does not stop after it has pointed, but continues, amplified, and sings as Jackie croons to her living glass that will do her will, and sings again as the crystal glitters and spins and points again, points again, and sings until Lena snatches the mere bottle off the pavement and by flinging it with all her force turns it into knives that slice too fast for the eye at Jackie's forehead but leave a flap of skin loose and the blood springing out and dropping like a veil over her eyes and she collapses into its black. With the girls petrified in their tableau the headmistress with the school doctor at her heels comes running from her office where they had at that minute been watching and wondering.

('Does she still bear those scars,' I wondered, 'is this the reason for her ever-veil?')

The doctor knelt over Jackie, who was coming round even as he touched her. Lena was starting to shake and sob. The headmistress went across and put her arm around her. Lena began to speak in a low grinding voice like the sound of a bottle spinning faster and faster. Her brittle voice became a shriek, then burst as glass will do. There were tears flung and fragmented as Lena shook her head from side to side.

'I killed her, I killed the witch, I cut her above the breath and destroyed her power!'

'Lena, Jackie's not dead or even badly hurt. That was a wicked thing to do, but as it turns out it's not as bad as it might have been.'

Bells rang. It was time for class. The playground cleared. Lena was led away to the staff common-room, which would be empty now, to rest. The doctor helped Jackie into his car. She seemed recovered, and the doctor had her press a large piece of lint to her wound until he got her to the surgery, where it would need stitches, and a handsome prominent turban of white bandages.

Later, he returned for a conference with the headmistress.

'We'll have to see how it heals. I don't think we'll need plastic surgery. If we do, it's simple enough. They can usually tuck a faint scar into a wrinkle-line.'

'I daresay! But young girls don't have wrinkles. I'll have to go straight round to see the parents. We'll be lucky if there's no suit.'

'Whose fault was it? Not yours surely. Lena shouldn't have come back to school so soon after the death.'

'We thought it better for her not to brood. I don't know where the fault lies. Human beings, I think. Jackie's situation is curious. You get these complaints against her and there's nothing tangible. She has fits of daydreaming. Most girls do at her age.

But when Jackie comes out of hers she makes a point of saying something. Her schoolfellows decide to take it as an oracle and trouble follows. They're saying now that she cursed Lena and caused the accident that killed Bob.'

'I'm sure that makes her feel important.'

'But it was Lena who actually committed the violence — on a rumour, an exaggeration, a supposition, no more. I expect Lena feels fully justified.'

'Surely she'll have to be suspended from school now.'

'Yes, perhaps until the summer. But it is Jackie who's the ongoing problem. She's not inherently unsociable, I think. A late developer, sure. Lonely. I want her to grow out of the situation she's got herself into here. But the silly creatures have started to call her "witch".'

'What about the girl I saw this morning? Sally. She admitted she had had a fright, then clammed up.'

'Didn't she tell you?'

'No.'

'She said she had seen Jackie in two places at once. It was in the library. Jackie was there reading quietly at a table near the window. Sally says Jackie looked at Sally and smiled her beautiful smile, then looked out of the window. Sally looked out too and swears there was another Jackie walking along the path outside. At first the head of the figure was bent and hair veiled the face. Then the Jackie outside threw her hair back and looked in at the Jackie inside. Then they both looked at Sally, smiling. Sally fainted, and when she came to the library was empty.'

'Sally wears glasses.'

'Precisely. And if she takes them off she's inclined to get double vision. But I can't get up in Assembly and recite a list of rational explanations for what is a social phenomenon. They have elected Jackie a witch and are making her a scapegoat for all the new strangenesses of their developing adolescent lives. The best I can do is to persuade Jackie that she's not a heroine and she's not to lay bait for her tormentors.'

'She'd understand, I think. She's not a dunce.'

'In a way that makes it worse. The girls have got something quite definite to be jealous about. Jackie never loses her poise. Actually she's not outstandingly good in any one subject —

except that once or twice in a term she has a flash of insight that astonishes her teachers.'

'She's intuitive.'

'And that is an excellent thing. I blame Jackie for nothing but the little occult gesture she affects when she wants to impress with her power. She fans her fingers a little, like this, and mutters a rhyme. I shall tell her that this is asking for exactly the kind of trouble she's got. Then she goes quiet and glassy eyed, and after a bit comes to with a particularly radiant smile, and delivers herself of whatever gem she's thought of in her little meditation.'

'Epilepsy,' says the doctor; 'some epileptic children fan their fingers across the sun or over the electric light to bring on fits — especially when they want to get out of something they're supposed to do. I had a patient who feared the wind blowing as others fear thunderstorms, and would not walk under trees for fear that the vibration of the branches over the sky or their shadows moving across his path would trip him into a fit. Some children enjoy the sensation, the "aura", and bring it on deliberately — their version of glue-sniffing. They say it makes the world glow, as if lit from inside, and pulse and stream with strange energies. Then most of them go too far, to the point of no return. They fall into unconsciousness over this invisible threshold, and the fit supervenes. One man had to give up studying the Bible in the original Hebrew. Reading from right to left brought on fits. For a time he was on the brink of religious mania. Called his fits "prophecies". They would always have a rotating disc, usually a potter's wheel, in the ancient slave-markets. Rotating it in front of a slave's eyes to check whether he was liable to fits. You can test for epilepsy by taking the back of the clock off and showing them the works inside.'

'No,' says the headmistress firmly, 'I don't think Jackie can be an epileptic. Our maths woman told me one of the most remarkable stories about Jackie. The class was learning how to use punch-button calculators. Miss Mason likes to surprise them with sums that jam the circuits with recurring numbers and make the calculator stick. Then the circuits have to be cleared. Certain square roots do that, as you know. Technically they're called "irrational numbers". "What's the square root of four, dears?" And all the dears punch up their figures good as gold and shout out the answer: "Two, Miss Mason." "Square root of nine?" "Three, Miss Mason." "Now the square root of seven, girls." "2.6457313111, Miss Mason," calls out Jackie with her extraordinary smile — or some such number — before the others have a chance. Then they put it on the calculators and she's right. Or so they say. Of course nobody thought beforehand of taking down the number she actually said. Moreover she recited more figures than the little calculators are able to print out. Pencil and paper would have clinched it.'

'I think most children have flashes of mental power they're seldom able to recover when they grow up,' I said.

'May I continue?' said Madame. 'There are questions of choice, sin and freewill involved, to say nothing of magical masturbation. That comes later.'

'I want to ask something else before we go on. That is the first time you've mentioned sin in this office or anywhere else so far as I know. Has any of us here, in the Institute, ever done anything really wrong — or are we all just victims?'

'I've been trying to tell you,' said Madame, 'everybody misbehaves. It's the best part of you. God misbehaves.'

'What about people who are really expert negative facilitators? Somebody who facilitates another's death, for example. One of my close friends here when he arrived thought he was a murderer. Now he thinks he has been murdered. But since murders create gods, it has made him religious. Now he's interested in resurrection. But should I fear him or anybody else here? Has anyone sent you a convicted murderer to live in?'

'That would be telling,' said Madame complacently.

I was shocked that the question of murder had come up. My marriage scenario had not so far included murder, but supposing she was as mean with her riches as she was with her presence, as elusive after marriage as before it? I would be jealous. Murder would keep her still. Something is murdered in everybody who gets married.

'Only remarkable facilitators get murdered, remarked Sir Geoffrey, 'and only the greatest of them survive it.' I seemed to see a warning glance flash between him and Madame, despite the veil. I was jealous of that glance. I thought of all the red blood in that black carcass. He showed me some by opening his mouth and laughing.

'That is something we like to leave to the parents,' says the headmistress.

Jackie's stepfather was beginning to get cross. 'You're telling me that my daughter is an excellent student and that she's done nothing wrong, but that she is a bad influence and must be made to leave your school.'

'Not exactly a bad influence.'

'Then what, exactly.' He is a minor local government official, and used to bullying clerks and dustmen. This is his first teacher. He likes the feeling of her in his teeth.

'The girls . . . they blame her for feelings they themselves have.'

'Then it's the other girls who are the bad influence. Why not expel them?'

'I cannot run a school for one student!'

('Can't she,' said Madame thoughtfully, 'can't she really!')

'One of those exemplary students that you run your school for threw a bottle at my girl and she had to have stitches. Is the girl who threw the bottle a good influence? Will you run your school for her and her ilk? Or will you tackle the problem of your gifted pupil? If that's what she is. Perhaps you will tell me that at your school gifted children are more trouble than they're worth?'

The headmistress has had enough of being bullied.

'Can we stop scoring points, for Jackie's sake. You're her father. She lives in this house, not in my school. Please be honest and tell me if you truly think there's nothing wrong at home and the school is solely to blame!'

There was a long pause. Then the stepfather spoke again.

'There are some decorations being done. Can you smell the paint? I'd like you to come and have a look.'

The headmistress is puzzled by this change of subject. She lets Jackie's father take her stealthily up the stairs. Once up the second flight, on Jackie's landing, he peers round the half-open door, from which a bright white light shines. He puts a finger to his lips, hushing her, and beckons. She looks into the room startled, turns round to Father, frowning. He repeats his gesture of silence. The room is sheerly white, like the inside of a seashell, and brightly lit with a white fluorescent lighting-strip. Jackie comes slowly into view, painting the exposed floorboards with a second coat of quick-drying gloss. Stepfather tugs at the headmistress's sleeve. He doesn't want Jackie to see them up there. Quietly they return downstairs.

Grannie and Jackie's mother are waiting for them in the lounge. The younger woman, Cecily, was a slim and lithe violet-eyed beauty when she was with David Dimitrios. Now she has grown dumpy and her hair is cut short, and the violet eyes move around the room cautiously, and no longer flash. Her new husband is a rest after the excitements of the old Institute. Somehow, as David's wife, the work there had not been explained to her, and it was a blow when she had understood that some of it involved his being unfaithful. He had had children by certain of his pupils or patients. Cecily remembered uneasily that there had been white rooms at that Institute too.

Stepfather is explaining about the room.

'When Cecily and Jackie came to me, they had had a hard time. We fitted up Jackie's room as nicely as we could. Wall-to-wall carpet to make it cosy, storage heater, lovely little brass bedstead. She's flung all that into the spare room. Now it's as you see it. She's even painted over the windows. In herself she's fine — except when you ask her about her room, or try to stop her. After what has happened at the school, I think it's the strain there. I don't know whether she's gifted or whether she's going round the bend. I know she has a gift for upsetting people. Can she see a bit further than the rest of us, or is it just sickness and,' he glances at Cecily, 'her background?' He decides to be cruel. 'She had a very curious background. Her father runs some kind of occult institute. Cecily and I don't believe this can be hereditary, but now I'm not sure. I hoped a good school would help.'

'Schooling only brings out whatever's there,' pronounces the headmistress, who has seen everything, except what's here.

'It's done that all right,' snaps stepfather.

'I think it's time to bring Jackie into all this. If she is under strain at school, it's because of the whispering and sidelong glances. Bring it out into the open. Talk about her "background" as you call it. She probably wants that. Talk about your own background. Trade secrets. You'll get her trust that way.'

Grannie passes her claw across her deeply lined forehead under the smooth waves of her steely-blue coiffure. 'Get Jackie to tell her own fortune, my dears,' says Grannie.

('This is where magical masturbation comes in,' said Madame. 'I thought you'd be interested.')

I'll call Jackie down, shall I?' says stepfather.

'No,' says her mother, 'I'll go up and get her.'

Jackie had turned the strip-lighting off in her white cave, and set a candle on a low white table in the middle of the room. This is the only remnant of furniture; it is just recognisable as the dressing-table with the mirror removed and the legs sawn off, repainted. Mother becomes a little dizzy as she enters the room, from the paint-smell.

'Won't you need a mirror, dear?' Cecily remembers the white room behind the conservatory at the old Institute, the bleached sheepskin rugs, the glass table, the white-clothed man called Simon with the terrifying smile — was he David's twin son?*

'No, Mother, I'd rather not have a mirror in here. There are just enough shadows.' The candlelight plays with their every movement, yellow and black, like a cave of grass, of tigers in the grass.

'Shouldn't we open the windows to get rid of that paint-smell?'

To her surprise Jackie smiles brilliantly.

'That's a good idea! We can't use the place while it smells like this.' She pinches out the candle and her mother helps her open the glossed-over windows. The catches are stuck with paint.

Downstairs, Jackie and her stepfather immediately started arguing. The headmistress had gone. She thought it best that the next round of talks should be a family affair. Jackie had taken an upright chair, with her parents ranged opposite her on the sofa. Grannie sat near the fire, the great mask of her coiffure rearing up every now and again as she nodded; like many old folk she seemed to live in a kind of seesaw rhythm, slipping in and out of sleep, or memories, on an undulant track. It looked like a trial scene, with Jackie in the upright dock, and her parents lower down in the jury-box. Jackie had not meant to arrange it like that, but she had. She usually talked sprawled on the floor, like a reasonable being.

She had to begin by protesting this very point.

*Please see *The Beekeepers by* Peter Redgrove (Stride, 2006).

'I'm not on trial. What does it matter to you what I do?'

'The headmistress is very worried . . .'

'We're very worried,' said mother.

'Doesn't it bother you at all that a schoolfriend wanted to kill you?'

'She's not a friend.'

'Catastrophes just follow you around.' Father was working up steam again.

'It's not my fault what the girls think.' Jackie is near tears.

'What do they think?'

'They say I'm a witch.' There's a pause here. A new kind of word has been employed within the family circle, a new dimension approaches. Father immediately becomes tentative. You use the good old words if you want to bawl out a head dustman; new words and concepts must be ventilated in committee, with every avenue explored. A wheedling note enters his voice.

'But, Jackie, you must be doing something to make them think that.'

There is another pause. A secret is coming. Some unspoken fact of life.

'It's only what everybody does. When they want to be happy.' There's no reply, so Jackie plunges on. If this be magic, it is lawful as eating. 'I touch myself, here and here,' she touches her skirt, her breasts, her hair lightly, quickly; 'I touch myself and I relax and I try to join up the places I touch so I can feel my whole shape. I try to feel my whole skin and my whole body. I feel I am breathing through my skin. It is warm and I enter it and I begin to dream a little in bright sudden pictures. There are people, events, friends walking about in their scenes. I watch them, and sometimes I can step in among them. Often the scenes are brightly lit, but if the light is slow in coming I make it flow by touching myself hard, here.' Stepfather's face is stony as Jackie touches her skirt in the front. 'When my skin is more open, all I need is the light of a candle. I gather it, like this.' She shows the fanning gesture. 'Or an electric light, but that is coarser, too mathematical. I see answers to school questions written sometimes, but often when I'm puzzled I forget to ask. When I really want something I concentrate on my wish by making it into a little rhyme. If I use dancing and singing, the people inside dance and sing too, and play, just as if they were children. Everybody there seems just the age they ought to be. You, Grannie, you're there, and Mother; David's there, but he's like a young boy. They've told us about this in sex-instruction at school, only they didn't tell us what it was really like. They used such an ugly word too: "Masturbation", and they said we weren't to be guilty, because everybody did this. I thought it was what you did when you didn't have another person to do it with, which was more advanced. So I thought I ought to do it a lot. It is nice, and it was teaching me, and when I did have another person to do it with, then I'd be very good at it.'

Stepfather is scarlet. The two older women are looking down at their laps; Grannie has stopped nodding.

'So it's the way Mummy made me with David, and the way she's going to make my brother or sister with Daddy. You make this magic light in you both, and it's strong enough to take food from Mummy's body, and it's a baby; and in that baby is a spark of the fire that made it, and that it must keep alight with magic. Just as I do. Grown-ups must be very good at it, since they've got each other. Mummy, it's true isn't it?'

Cecily is beginning to speak as her husband jumps in.

'Now look here, Jackie . . .'

'I don't mind saying . . .' Cecily is going to speak and the man gives way.

'Yes, I don't mind saying. I don't know why we keep it dark, but we do. Living pictures.' She turns fondly to the man, and he avoids her eyes. 'Memories of happy times we have spent together, sharp and vivid, when he touches me, when he's loving. As though the times we've spent were somehow electrically photographed in my skin, and his hands closed a circuit, and the pictures leapt to the surface. I can wear them then. He clothes me in them, our life joins together. David did this too, but the pictures were darker, a little unhappy sometimes when the album in my skin turned living pages. When you came, Jackie, it was as though one of the living pictures had walked out of the happier pages. I seemed to recognise you like a memory coming back to one, even when you were a little baby. I loved to nurse you by candlelight. It was like a waking dream.'

Father is staring hard at the carpet.

'If you can't love yourself, how can you love another?' remarks Grannie.

'You were like my other self, Jackie. And, when I married again, so was father.'

She looks at him, and touches his rigid shoulder.

'Oh Cecily, what can I say? Until you said that, I was thinking that you were all raving loonies. As a mere man, that is. All I can say is that I love you in the best way I can. Until you spoke, I hadn't really understood whether I had succeeded or not.'

'That's all right, then.' Grannie has perked up. 'So long as it's not just Jackie. I've been ashamed and worried. All I could think of was that it was wrong for Jackie to grow up strange, so I said nothing, even though I knew I was the same. My own Grannie taught me a little rhyme and how to see moving pictures in the fire, or in the snow falling, or in the shadows of the candle. When I grew up, I still loved to do this, but it was stronger now, since the life in my imaginings was increased by the pleasure it gave me to touch myself, to be touched, to touch.

'Dick, my first husband, hated all that. One day he caught me in what he called my "solitary vice". He hit me so hard I fell on the floor and when I was down he ground his heel into the hand I used to gather my living light. This hand.'

She holds out the gnarled and useless arthritic claw. She has been sitting primly, with hands in lap, and feet together. Now she spreads her legs under the full tweed skirt, tucks her crippled hand deep in that lap, and closes her legs around it.

'My Grannie used to say that if you could see your own left hand in a dream, then you had power over your fate. After Dick had spoilt it, and it was in splints, I had a dream of him getting into his car to go away. I lifted up my hand to wave to him, and it was my left hand, and it was uninjured, so I forgot Dick in my pleasure at this. A few days later Dick was drunk and drove off in an angry mood and I did not lift a finger to stop him. He ran his car off the road into a tree and burned to death.

'Oh, I wished him no ill. I let him go and do as he wanted as an example to him, simply because he would not let me be my own self. These things have a way of working themselves out. I had told nobody about my dream, so nobody accused me of being a murderess and a witch simply because my dream had told me to be myself, heal myself. Dick had nailed up the little schoolroom which was my quiet room, where he had caught me at my finger-prayer. Your Granddad, Jackie, he was a good man. He pulled the nails out of the door when we married and I had my dusty little room again. It was soon back to normal. I turned it into the nursery, and then into a school-room again. I taught you the rhymes, Cecily, and how to have a quiet time; I did not dare to teach you how to touch yourself, though I wanted you to learn this. I knew when you began to, and I was pleased, and you felt my approval. When you married that brooding, brilliant Dr Dimitrios — well, I was pleased at that too. I knew he was a witch or a magician, and I thought you would learn from him more than I had in my life, and you would bring lightness and love to his studies. He was a greedy man, and the study itself enlarges virtues, monstrifies faults. I should have spoken out, named our Craft, called you "witch" and made you proud of that; then he might have accepted you as an equal in his work, and you would have been prepared for what was involved. This work that I speak of is an alchemy to find the stone that turns the world to gold. The beginnings of it are in that light that you see in your body.

'So, Jackie, now I must do my duty. I do call you to your Craft, I call you Witch, and bid you seek your fortune. You've done enough fortune-telling for other people. Too much, as you've found out. Now you must tell your own. It has been working in you of itself. You have made your workroom. You have made a place between the worlds. You must seek your fortune of the Lady.'

The three women are radiant. The glow in their skins of pleasure seems to the stepfather a foreshadowing or metaphor of that rumoured light in the skin of their strange story. He has been quite spellbound; images of his boyhood keep popping into his head; there is a cricket match and a special friend, transformed by his whites, kissing him; is it a memory or a wish; oh, he remembers, he wishes his friend were Jesus. Cecily gets up and takes his hand.

'Eh?' says stepfather. 'I'm not sure I like this. What are we doing now?'

'It's a kind of seance, dear,' says Cecily. 'Come along.'

'To find out what to do.' He's pleased at the taking up of a definite course of action. 'Of course. Come along.'

'Do I give the Lady a name?' asks Jackie.

'Yes,' says Grannie. She has just been to see a famed musical comedy. 'Call her Madame.' Smiling, Grannie begins to unpin her gigantic hair, takes a comb from her pocket.

Upstairs in Jackie's white den, the women are able to tuck their limbs in, in various ways, and sit quite naturally at the low white table. The candle is alight in its holder, but the flame is almost drenched invisible by the strong glare bouncing from the walls and the blank window-frame, light dissolved in light. Stepfather is a trifle stout and finds squatting not comfortable; he makes the best of a bad job with legs stretched out and arms propping him.

'Lights, dear,' says Mother.

'Lights. Righto.'

The room is suddenly pitch dark, then yellow candlelight and its flickering shadows prancing and plucking blooms in their eyes; the tigerish cave of grass reassembles itself. Father watches the shaggy shadows of the women thrown on the wall behind them, and thinks that this is how the cave paintings were made, by such a light in such a cavern — though this is two floors up in a suburban villa. Did the ancient inhabitants of the caves see the spirits of animals in the shadows conjured up at seances like this, but deep in the mountain, presided over by women exercising their prerogatives and mysteries, the perks of the man being the oh-so-vivid essence of the hunger's animal, captured in its very bone outline in his mind, so exact to the animal's nature that the vision imprinted spontaneous hunting skills, the outline of this insight echoing down time? As the light of this paraffin candle echoes down time, it is sunlight captured by the plants of the Coal Age, sealed under the rock and the seas for millennia, now released at the tip of the wick wrapped in the grease of those plants' decay.

'When you consult the light in your skin concerning future events, what exactly do you see? Tell me, Jackie.' Grannie has combed all the lacquer out of her steely hair, and it lies down her back streaming like a deep river with a ripple in it, all that is left of the complicated cerebral convolutions of her usual Janus-head. 'Tell me exactly.'

'I see a round light, and it grows clearer as I touch myself in my place. Against this cool light I see a shape. It's like a mound, but as it is shadowed by the light behind it, cutting into the luminous disc, I can't make it out very clearly. Then it nods, as if it is ready for me. It is a very strange image, because at the same time as I begin to see it, my climax comes, and under my hand I feel my womb nod behind my triangle of hair. After that climax, I feel a warmth, and a warm glow comes into the picture too. I try to place this new light in the space between myself and the nodding mound, so I can see it clearly. I put it there in the shape of my candle, and I fan my hand in front of the flame of my here-and-now candle to make the light lively. Then I stop, and let the inner candle glow steadily so that it shines on the mound.'

'What do you see?'

'It is a veiled woman. She answers my questions by nodding or shaking her head. I have never seen her face.'

'Make yourself like this woman.'

Jackie wants to get at the drawer in her sawn-off dressing-table. By means of wriggling and shifting, they manage to open it, and Jackie rummages there. She pulls out a long piece of black mesh, closes the drawer, places the veil over her head, the only still shadow in the room. The scent of the candle-flame is like a zest in the air.

Jackie is now fanning her hands across the candle-flame, and the shadows whirl. It is as though she is stirring a pool of gold and black wriggling fish, or starting a wheel moving. She allows the gesture to expand and extend until, now, she is stroking her thighs, her stomach, her breasts, her throat. To stepfather's incredulous gaze, his wife, Cecily, godly matron of forty-five years of age, joins in her daughter's sultry self-stimulation, and the same radiant smile blooms on the young and the middle-aged; and Grannie watching them is smiling too, and she begins to stimulate herself like a teenager, stroking her forehead with her uninjured hand, and applying the hard pebbliness of her arthritic knuckles to her important place between her spread legs. The breath of the women comes faster, and the wheel of shadows whirls faster; then the breath catches and pulls in, and pulls in again like mounting a staircase to a giddy height; then the triple sigh comes with a great relaxed 'Aaaah' ending in a light hum:

'Aaaaahuuum'; and in a little the madly whirling flame steadies and glows stilly, the shadows trembling in their places. The eyes of the unveiled women are closed, Jackie is unmoving behind her veil. Father watches with bright scared eyes in pouches and a sharp nose.

('Veiled and still,' says Madame, 'as I am. Would you see my face?' She throws back her veil and looks round at us. Her face is dead white, painted like a Kabuki mask, with high black eyebrows and crimson lips. She takes out matches and lights the candle in its pewter holder on the table in front of her. I cross and turn out the standard lamp. Madame replaces her veil. This room is pitch dark, before the candle-glow blooms as it does in that other room, which is touching ours now.)

'Can you see the figure, Jackie?'

Jackie's veiled head nods.

'Tell your fortune. Ask it your questions.'

'Is it my fate to tell fortunes?' asks Madame in Jackie's young voice; then, after a pause, she shakes her veiled head slowly.

'Shall I be seen everywhere, is that my quality, to be famous?'

The veiled head shakes slowly.

'These glimpses of mental power. These mathematics. Is this my sole talent?'

The veiled head shakes slowly.

'Am I to be wealthy? Is this my destiny?'

The veiled head shakes slowly.

'Is my talent sexual, will my career be to inspire with these energies?'

The veiled head shakes slowly.

'Am I merely an artist, a painter of pictures, of word-cadences or music?'

The veiled head shakes slowly.

There is a catch in Jackie's voice as these doors are closed by her vision.

'Am I to be a healer, and that is to be my direction?'

The veiled head shakes slowly. Jackie begins to fear the reason.

'Am I to die young, before I can become what I am?'

The veiled head shakes slowly. It isn't death that will prevent her.

'Will I have a family, and give myself to it; is that my nature?'

The veiled head shakes slowly.

There is no hope. She has used her magic. It brings her nullity. The universe is empty. She is to do nothing, be nothing. The depths are empty. She is cut off from all she had thought was in her. The figure has said 'I never knew you.'

Then she asks in a whisper, 'Is it all these things?'

Grannie's claw eases and opens, and slides in its bones, and becomes a hand.

The veiled head nods three times, quickly.

* * * * *

I sprang to my feet and thumped with my fist on Madame's desk.

'I want some of this! Why should you be the only one with gifts? I want to be a medium, I want to call up ghosts. If necessary I will create my own, by suicide. Or murder. In fact I'm going to do a murder. I'm going to murder white.' I swung on Sir Geoffrey. 'You needn't think you're always going to be the only black man here. I've got ectoplasm too — more black plasm than anybody here. I'm immensely rich with plasm. *And* it is black, all shining black! I can journey among the dead if you can. And return.' There! I had opened the black coffers of harvest at last.

Madame got up, and touched my hand. 'I know. You want to dance.'

I was amazed that she seemed to understand. It was the next card to be played; all's fair, I said to myself. My plot was to marry her. Very well, I must declare my own dark dowry, as sure as my name was Xavier.

* * * * *

Dan was full of information about the bees. He told me how, when Madame returned to her real father, David Dimitrios had turned the whole Institute over to bee-disciplines. This was how Dan had got his training; though it was the saddest time of his life when he lost his twin in the explosion.

Dimitrios had taught his daughter, and she had become a

superlative bee-master. They would spend long hours staring into the open hives, perched on high stools as if reading books together. The refectory tables were polished with beeswax and during meals lighted with candles of beeswax: sheets of the hexagon-embossed wax rolled round the spluttering wicks. It was a tradition followed to this day in the new Institute, and there was the faint pervasive taste of beeswax in all the food. There were sessions of many hours using the candles in a meditation called 'trataka'; it was said that the sibilant sputtering of the wick was the speech of the spirits: the actual sound, hissing and spitting, like an energetic whisper of a running man passing you in the dark, whether or not a named spirit was present. That sound, and the hum of the bees.

It became the habit of the old Institute under David to evoke at every opportunity the cycles of nature, energy pouring from the great fountain of the sun, and passing through all the forms of nature. The common greeting consisted in the tracing of a circle in the air with the left forefinger, and a soft buzz pronounced with the lips lightly compressed and smiling. Significances were expounded by a Petar or Shower, usually David, in one of the white rooms. A hive was brought in, and uncapped, while the audience was seated, and the bees explored the white spaces, every one visible like an intense seed of winged energy. The audience would sit there, the initiates in bee-costume, holding hands with the white-clad 'humans', as the novices were called, hand in hand, alternate, bee-human, bee-human. Initiates would hum in an under-bass as the sermon was delivered by the Petar, of how the plants drank up the sunshine, and the bees made their wax from the plants, and so the candles stored up the blessed sunshine itself, and gave it back in the house at night, and it behoved all to wash their faces in the beautiful candlelight before sleeping, and to dream in candlelight as the bee-food eaten slowly released a like light in their minds; that each person was a kind of candle of honey, burning at both ends, the head a veiled flame, and energy travelling up the wick, which was the spine, from the molten pool of honey digested in the viscera, clean as folded laundry from the vegetarian diet, and not stinking like a dog's bowel from forbidden meat. The sermon was delivered in a special high-humming holy voice; all capable of it would endure the sermon in a light doze; this was the purpose of the training, to learn trance-listening: what was said was not merely heard, but seen, like listening to Saturday-night theatre on the radio in bed. At the end of the session, dark bees were knocked into a basket from the white clothes of the novices; one earned merit by the count of bees that had been attracted to one's clothes. After this, the exhausted novices filed out for their tea of bread-and-honey.

In this manner David Dimitrios and Jackie his daughter taught that bees are the mirror of nature. Further initiation was obtained by contemplation of the rustling, humming, multi-scaled mirror of bees-wings of the hive. Even the future could be seen in the glittering of wings. Hence the hours spent staring into the hives, perched high like tennis-umpires, one's scribe perched near at standby, in case of important prophecies. Madame often prophesied, and it was said published the resulting scripts under a pseudonym as poetry. There were also healing-sessions. Dan told me about a particularly interesting one he attended where a handsome old woman with long steely-grey hair and beautiful supple hands, whom Madame addressed as Grannie, was teaching a mixed class of arthritics to masturbate by using the joints of their badly deformed fingers. It was a great cure, apparently, to use that which gave pain for one's pleasure; the joints usually eased after a few sessions and the swelling reduced immediately. I did not believe all Daniel's stories. He said that everybody kept remarkably healthy, and they would saturate their bodies with bee-products; all would go on periodic diets of nothing but pollen, propolis and royal jelly; on special occasions the women caught up their hair in elaborate convoluted bee-hive coiffures, dressing them with honey and wax. Daniel said that these hairdos were made to look like great faces of beeswax from the back, which would rear up regally in counterpoise to the woman's lowering her face in front demurely, flirtatiously.

Now Daniel grew more serious as he told me about the terrible accident in the pub. It was after the sad death in the Institute of a gifted psychic, who had once been a poet; after his funeral a terrorist bomb planted in a rucksack in the saloon bar where they were drinking the poet's farewells exploded under their table, and smashed David and some of his associates, including

* See Peter Redgrove: *The Beekeepers* (Stride, 2006)

Daniel's twin. Daniel was there, but his body was shielded by the table.*

'You must have sustained injuries . . .' He looked pleased at my doubt.

'Madame ignored her grief and took me in hand,' he said; 'yes, I have healed well, but the scars are always visible, to everyone, and they are not of the kind that I can ever forget . . .'

'The scars . . . what scars . . . I see no scars!'

'You dear man! Did you think I was born a dwarf?'

A full eighteen inches of macerated tissue, nerve and blood-vessel had had to be removed from both legs. The bone-grafts took so well that he was soon able to walk. With the help of yoga and physiotherapy, together with the Institute's healthy diet and healing-sessions, which included psychotherapy, he had done so well, and acquired such an extensive knowledge of techniques proved upon his own body, that Madame appointed him yoga-master and physiotherapist at the new Institute. There was a sudden influx of money from somewhere, and Madame was able to buy the whole Cornish tongue of land on which the present Institute stood. It was said that Madame buried what was left of David, making him up into a whole body with pieces of his associates and fellow-drinkers, in a tank of honey, and that the fragmented person of David was still floating in bits secreted somewhere in the Institute, in a place known only to her. Sometimes she went there, it was rumoured, if extremely difficult problems arose, and consulted his floating lips, rubbing clear the glass window she had caused to be set in the tank and shining her lantern into the darkening honey to glimpse the white hair and blown-off face that swam and spoke to her.

Madame had changed the regime after the accident.

Water entered much more into the various curative programmes, and mud. My ears pricked up at that, as I knew a little about mud. I wondered how much of Daniel's story was true, and how much his self-healing fantasy; if he had been injured, whether it had been in that exalted Dimitrian company; or whether he was here to get over being a red-haired dwarf. He said that when Madame was away he taught the breathing exercises that were based on the bee-disciplines. If I could observe the degree of his skill, that would help me decide about his story.

'I would like to learn this breathing.'

'You shall one day, but my class is for young people.'

'Couldn't I join in? I would need to learn it all from the beginning.'

'They aren't beginners. They're very advanced. They've been learning the movements since they were toddlers.'

'Will Madame teach me?'

'I don't know about that . . .' he said abruptly. What was this sensitivity on the part of the staff about their chief? I began to wonder guiltily whether they had somehow divined my purpose here — to marry her. Was I talking in my sleep? It was quite likely that such a place did monitor and bug people's sleep.

'But you can come and watch if you like,' said Daniel.

* * * * *

Wrote Sir Geoffrey:

The pornographic archives guarded by bees
Who have built comb in the safe; iron doors
From which the honey drips; I sip a glass
Of bee-sherry, yellow and vibrant; I came here
Past the old post-office, boarded up,
From within the cool darkness sun-razored
I heard the hum of bees; my friend tells me

That the radioactive cities of the future
Will be left standing for euthanasia,
They will be kept beautiful though all trees
And lawns will be plastic. Those who wish to die
Will drift through the almost-empty streets,
Loiter through the windows of the stores,
All open, all untended, what they fancy they can take,
Or wander through the boulders of Central Park, its glades,
To hear the recorded pace and growl in the empty
zoo-cages,
And consider the unperturbed fountains of water,

While it, and they, are rinsed through and through
As the pluming spray by sunlight, with killing rays,
Lethal broadcasts, until they can consider no more.
Germs over the whole skin die first, the skin after,
Purity first, then death, in the germless city that amazes
The killed lovers with its pulsing night-auroras.

I reply I would prefer a city constructed of OM,
A city of bees, I want this disused city
Converted to a hive, all the skyscrapers
Packed with honeycomb, and from the windows
Honey seeping into the city abysses, all the streets
Rivers of cloudy honey slipping in tides,
And the breeze of the wings as they cool our city.

This would be my euthanasia, to be stung by sweetness,
To wander through the droning canyons scatheless at first,
Wax thresholds stalagmited with honey-crystals
I snap off and munch, and count the banks
That must brim with the royal jelly . . .

And some wander through the sweet death, city of hexagons,
And are not stung, break their hanging meals off cornices
In the summer-coloured city, drink at the public fountains
Blackened with wings drinking, and full of wonder
Emerge from the nether gates that are humming
Having seen nature building;
                                        others stagger
Through the misshapen streets, screaming of human glory,
Attended by black plumes of sting,
With a velvet skin of wings screaming they're flayed.

* * * * *

Daniel offered me a chair just outside the exercise area. The gym was large, white, airy. There were about sixty boys ready for exercise, dressed in close-fitting skullcaps and short dusky yellow-and-brown jackets. The sleeves of the latter were tight-fitting and banded with the colours, suggesting on the thin little arms insectile joints. Several elbows, in fact.

Daniel's costume was similar to the boys', except that he and some of the older ones (who towered over him) were wearing a kind of gold-painted sword.

'What are the big patch-pockets on the trouser legs?' I asked.

'They stand for the pollen-sacs,' answered Daniel.

'This is a very elaborate uniform for village boys whose parents I suppose don't have much cash!'

'Madame subsidises the course. Besides, a Mother will always find a way if it's a question of uniforms.'

'There's one thing missing, though.'

'What is that?'

'Why, Daniel, the wings!'

The wings are invisible when the bee is flying.'

'These boys are not flying.'

'Flying, in a sense, is the purpose of the exercises we teach.'

'These are David Dimitrios's exercises.'

'In part, though, they were in detail devised by Madame.'

'May I see your sword?'

'It is a sharpened rush that has been painted with a gold hilt and amber blade. We call it a "sting". It is purely symbolic.'

'Only you yourself and some of the older boys are wearing them.'

'You have to earn your sting.'

'But surely it is the drone which is the virile male, and drones have no stings.'

'It is the workers which have the stings, and the workers are maiden bees. They cannot be anything else. They have no reproductive apparatus. They are a species of eternal spinster. Sexless, as the angels are said to be . . .' '. . . or like the castrati of the medieval Vatican.'

'Now what are you getting at! I assure you that you would find any of my fully trained boys most formidable.'

'I am only trying to learn, Daniel.'

'Then let me tell you a thing or two. Or better, show you.' He raised his voice. 'NOW BEES!' Bees, I noted, not boys. 'NOW BEES, LET ME HEAR YOUR WINGS!'

At this all the boys simultaneously took a big breath, and started humming. I noticed that, in taking their breath, their bellies swelled first, and then their chests, as if they were filling up from the navels with air. This extra load of air taken in by the yogic 'complete breath', explained the vibrancy of the hum, which I could feel through the soles of my feet, and the length of time they were able to sustain the note. Daniel had begun by taking breath himself, and giving the boys a note, as the oboe in an orchestra that is tuning up gives an A. Daniel's, so far as I could estimate, was a low E. The smaller boys were ranked in front of the larger, as in a school photograph. The little ones ran out of breath first, and took their second breath while the big boys were still humming, so theoretically the sound would never need to cease.

Daniel took me by the hand and led me over to the humming boys. He put my hand on the skullcap of a little fellow in the front row — I snatched it away! The hum vibrated through my hand as if I had touched a big gong that was still ringing, or one of those buzzers practical jokers used to fasten to their palms to give a surprise handshake. Gingerly I put one finger back on top of the velvet pate. It was an agreeable sensation, full of life. The boy grinned up at me cheerfully, still humming.

I returned to my chair. Daniel was about chin-height to me when I was seated. He wore a military demeanour here, and looked every inch the angry little bee in his costume, the red hair bristling under the skullcap, like fire boiling a pot. He embarked on a speech I thought he had given several times before.

'*Apis mellifica,* the honey-bee, vibrates its wings 200 times a second, 12,000 times a minute. It is this vibration which causes the energetic hum. Human boys cannot use the muscles of their limbs in any such fashion as the honey-bee does. There is only one way they can make such vibrations — with their little windpipes and lungs, and the resonating cavities and sinuses in their chest-bones and foreheads. The hum, correctly taught and practised, is very beneficial to their physiology and development. The inhalations are even and deep. The air, with its enriching oxygen, and its mysterious vital principle, *prana,* is retained for a period of time correct according to tradition. On a prolonged exhalation, the vibration massages all the internal organs. The boys get what you would call "high" quite naturally without recourse to drugs, alcohol, tobacco or girls. This is how they "fly".

Listen, and allow the note and the patterns of its resonance to form images within you, and you will learn meditation as David and Jackie Dimitrios taught it. "By means of the bees," as the great Bee-Doctor used to say, "we concentrate the ecstatic forces within us, into winged thoughts. Such thoughts form wonderful images in the honeycomb of the brain".' Daniel was watching the class intently.

'No, no, Bees, that is not good. You will not earn your stings that way. I will turn on the tape-recording. You must take your pitch from that, the alert but contented hive, ready to expel predators.'

'So you use a tape-recording to train them?'

'These are the recorded sounds of Dr Dimitrios's own original hives. You will hear the recordings change their key and pitch according to the emotions of the hive under attack, in warm sunshine, or in driving sleet.'

'Are the hives outside not the same colonies?'

'These recordings were made in the early days, when the strain was still pure, when the teaching was still pure.' To the Boy-bees: 'Now the angry wounded hive. Follow it, Bees! Assume the fighting-stance.'

All the little black bees-knees suddenly bent in a crouch and the little gloved knuckles tightened in gleaming fists. I suddenly thought of Sir Geoffrey's remark about WASPs, and how by that he must have meant fascists.

'Why, Daniel, these are martial arts!'

'Only when necessary. When there is an intruder, an enemy of the hive. You are not an enemy of their hive, are you?' The little man had grown terribly excited.

'But you said they were meditating! The boys are marching forward phalanx by phalanx, hitting out at the empty air, humming.' The mellow E had turned to an urgent B flat.

'And if any of those blows landed, they would break bone, they would sting!'

'You said it was a meditation-class.'

'Each boy strikes his opponent without anger, and with perfect stillness in his heart.'

'I don't suppose that's much comfort to the injured.'

'Those who breach the sanctity of the hive deserve suffering, they deserve to be torn to pieces by the bees, torn by the bees . . .' He broke into humming again and the boys advanced on us in humming waves, breaking ranks, turning, and reforming behind, and coming again. I could hear above the humming the faint whistle of the blows given with stiffened hand, like sword-strokes in the air.

'The hive? What is the hive?'

'Why, what else but this peninsula of rock, this Institute, the village, the docks, this private world.'

The vibration all around was making me feel light-headed. Daniel bent towards me confidentially.

'You are mad, aren't you?' I nodded my head dumbly. 'Of course you are. Why would you be here otherwise? Well, you shall be recovered here, or else here it will not be noticed in you, among your fellow-facilitators. Yet there is a stigma, having once been mad. You may have to defend yourself against detractors. You must carry yourself well. These boys live hard by the madhouse, in the village that belongs to it. They will perchance need to defend their self-respect against the wit of neighbouring boys. I am giving them madhouse training for life on the outside! And I shall show you how they adore the Queen!'

'They sprint and spring forward and back, and their little striking fists are blurred like wings with the speed of their strokes. Daniel, do you have control of these boys?'

'Hadn't you better hum, and do as I do? Watch this. Now, class, the loyal salutation. Bees, the Queen.'

The class spoke as though the hive had one voice, bristle-bearded and resonant, the words as if made out of the humming of wings: 'MADAME — GOD BLESS HER MAJESTY!' It was like a God of the Bees speaking. Then there was a dead silence, and I realised they were looking at me.

'God Bless Madame indeed,' I said hastily, 'wherever she may be.' Daniel eyed me at that, and I wished I had not added the last part.

'That fragrant breath from healthy lungs cools the hive, does it not?' demanded Daniel. I nodded, worried. I did not want to be torn to pieces. 'Do you not feel the zest in the air, like the smell of bees?' I was fed up with it in the cooking, but, yes, there was a pleasant lift to the air, as though it were lighted by many candles. So I nodded agreement again. 'Do you really understand our bee-ing? These Bees are restless" . . . They are not sure of you yet. You must pass our test. Bees, is he one of us?' They were all looking at me in the silence, and now a low hum started again, threateningly. 'Is he an intruder who will contaminate us? Bees, smell out this intruder with your feelers!' He stood aside and pointed at me.

Before I had a chance to move, the boys were upon me, in a hard-elbowed, granite-knuckled tide. They bowled me over and the chair I sat on; lying on my back with my legs still involved with the chair, I braced myself for pain and mutilation. But instead — excruciating torment — they went for my ribs and my ticklish places with their strong little fingers rippling like wavelets, and where there were fingers to spare, they tickled each other, laughing and rolling over me, and I laughed and screamed in protest, and felt a certain hard knuckle capable of delivering a particular blow forming in my trousers. This I tried to keep away from the boys' bodies as I rolled over and over with them, laughing; I wanted to enjoy the tickling without revealing my arousal; yet they didn't care, and I felt their hard little rods or stings and saw them too pressing against the material of their tight bee-knickerbockers, and behind it all glimpses of Daniel's face grinning. Yet despite this reaction, there was no sex in it; it was sensuousness and exhilaration, but not desire; and they were not cruel, they did not tickle me beyond enduring, but to see my helpless pleasure; and the other thing I enjoyed was the zestful pure breath that came out of their mouths. It smelled beautiful, like fresh-baked bread, with honey on it.

Eventually I struggled up, laughing still, dishevelled, exhausted, glowing, sidling my way to the exit, a little crouched, partly to protect my ribs from further tickling, partly to conceal my erection, though it was really too late for that; scuttling crabwise, waving pleasantly to Daniel to show I was all right, he watching me go, his arms akimbo, nodding like some gnome in the garden with its head on a pivot, like some pantomime dwarf watching Baron Hardupp amusingly and harmlessly discomfited in Mother Gooseland where all ferocity was play, just part of the fun. I pushed my way through the spring-loaded doors into the fresh air. My clothes were open and my trousers half-down. There was a fizz in my skin, as after a good swim and a rub-down! Why — I was the perfect fool of the Institute. I had been raped by a spirit yet again.

* * * * *

It began again immediately after the seance, when I had been raped by the spirit. I had not intended to bring my dance here. After all, if everyone danced their dance in the open view, there would be no time for the amenities, the shared rituals, and no opportunity, spinning our meaning out of our bodies continually, like gossamer spiders in May, spilling it. This dance of mine was something of a liability, it was too complicated, or if not that, too cumbersome. I would not reveal my dance to Madame until after I had married her, if it had not gone away by then. I thought of the great murderers, and how they kept their dance secret until the proper time.

I went with Sir Geoffrey down to the harbour to watch the reclaiming works. As a concession to the daylight, he wore a big white shirt, like a plain caftan, but his feet were bare. I saw how the black skin was rubbed to creaminess by the chafe of the earth. We strolled back towards the village.

'The Avenue of the Giants,' he said pleasantly, waving his arms under the big trees.

I looked up at them, as if for the first time. The light was winking between their leaves like innumerable eyes, opening and closing so that a certain number were open all the time, maintaining vision. A breeze passed, and I saw them breathing, like open lungs of green. The beauty and the sweetness of their breath was part of our walk, and part of my love for this man, as we talked. I thought, I have come here because I need to marry a certain woman, but also because I have a dance. Here, it will not be noticed in me. Here, my dance will not be mocked. I can perform it without penalty or ridicule.

We stopped for a drink at the Falling Leaf Tavern. The beer was the colour of autumn. Geoffrey showed me a poem he had written on his last visit, with used beer.

AUTUMN LUNCH

The lamp burns in the frosty
Glass roof of the lavatory
As the sun in a clouded sky.

These are autumn smells.
Gold liquors lash away from ourselves
Into deep sewers and wells.

We are russet-cheeked and severe,
Pompous with much golden-brown beer.
Now the landlord has bolted his door

We stagger away as the beer leads
Puffed up like trees in a breeze,
And rustle asleep deep in leaves.

We visited the church too, with the font of surprising water. A sprinkling of dust-grains over the surface made visible the constant slow wheeling of the holy water in the stone basin.

We climbed to the hill behind the church and looked down on the village streets below, simply a main road forking in two. Geoffrey pointed to the north, where the Institute gleamed like a pillared iceberg.

The dancing-ground made a level plateau of the hill. Geoffrey told me that it was a discalced ground, that for years it had never been touched by a clothed foot. He walked straight out on to the hard-packed earth and practised a few steps, pirouetting, his head turned up, laughing sideways, and winking. I struggled with my laces and socks, joined him. The dance-packed earth was almost dustless, and warm to the foot. Columns of bonfire-smoke climbed spiralling out of the villagers' gardens, and stood tall in the still air round about our vantage point, like spectators.

Then we climbed down and walked along the beaches to the tidal inlet. The tide was low and we strolled by flat sheets of black mud, watery earth, earthy water. Secretly I heard the first steps of my dance. As we returned, warm light glowed from the windows tunnelled under thatches. We passed a smouldering bonfire deep within which, as in a cage, mice of fire raced.

Geoffrey had taken off his white shirt, and was almost invisible in the dusk. His white eyes flashed above me, and his frequent smile. The white shirt fluttered from his fist.

Later, I dressed myself very carefully, for the dawn. My white shirt was spotless, its revers ironed smoothly open, a red scarf tucked in the opening, my trousers immaculate white. A broad black belt cuts my body in half. I carry a long peeled withy. Like a cricketer I am white; like a dancer, ready for my morris. I travel down the hill in the dark; dingy whites and greys manifest in the sky; there is a sudden gasp from the horizon full of the smell of tidal water. I hurry towards the mud.

I stand on the brink of the capacious mud. The floor of my dance has been prepared by the salt tide, swept and polished. I snuff up the strong perfume of the mud, like new-baked bread and fresh sawdust. As though my excitement were a bright light, my senses sharpen. The dawn indicates with one straight ray through a cloud my dancing-floor, glossy as chocolate.

I take my first step into the shallows. It is soft as drifted flowers, but an undersurface holds firm. As I step, I see the first beat of the great mud-drum ripple to the shore. There is a scent out of it of all the flowers not yet grown, the musk of marsh. It is dark as the grave, yet it is the cradle of grasses.

The plasm is firm though quaking. I mark my reflection out on the queasy mirror with my withy and my footsteps. Here is the way I dance my figure. First I lean out as far as I can stretch. Then with the tip of my withy I mark out two broad crescents, bulging towards me. They are the eyebrows. With a cry I leap over the eyebrows, and land steady astride up to my ankles. Thus are the pupils printed. Standing as I am, I mark the eye-sockets with my stick, upper and lower lids. Carefully I step over these lines and with a slithering step, my legs a little apart, mark the double lines of the long nose, which I finish by stamping out the nostrils. My footprints are the teeth of the smiling mouth a pace away. I enclose these features in a smooth circle scribed by my long wand.

Now I stamp out the trench of the throat. The mud grows swiftly deeper, yet my upper body is scarcely splashed, though the legs of my trousers are dipped in night; I wriggle my toes in the luxurious yeastiness. Now I dance with careful balancing gestures and excavating tread, the left and right arms of the great figure. With a spring I am knee-deep in two nipples, whose breasts I inscribe. I hop with feet pressed together into the navel, and from this mid-point I mark outlines of chest and ribs. With another leap I dance-delve down the midriff the long cunt. I scoop, I furrow, I dance its extent again and again; in its name I am dark to my belt. I hop to the hip and dance down the figure towards the sun to make an outstretched leg, returning to the cunt. I dance a right leg towards the sun, returning to the cunt. Hip-deep in the cunt (for when I am still, I sink deep) I fasten with my withy-tip hands to the wrists that grasp and spread that cunt.

Now I take a great bound and stand steady in the outlines of the feet, facing the sun that has risen, and is shining brightly on to the browny-gold ground. I sink slowly, and know full well that I shall be head-over if I stay, but see over my shoulder that my creature lies streaming out behind me like my own shadow. I pluck my feet out with difficulty and turn to face her, like my image in a black mirror, my left foot in her right, her left foot accepting my right. The sun behind me casts my shadow into the outline prepared for it. And now it is time to step over the threshold of my looking-glass into the black land, glass-land. I can never catch that moment of crossing. However long I linger on this side, I cannot slow that passage. One moment, I am my own self; the next, hers.

I am face-down, and I am with her! I have vaulted her boundaries and I am as black as she is. I am buried in her musky flesh; the blackness is merely the colours of all the flowers that are in it mingled together, and the bees in the flowers. It smells of wet feathers and mouldering leather. It shall pull through the flower-seed, like a black velvet pulled through the conjurer's ring to become his painted cloth and his moths and doves fluttering.

I pull the flesh of my lady off her form and clothe myself in it. I am the medium covered in the black ectoplasm that materialises the lady. I pour the cool mud over myself in thick veils, I mask myself, I dress myself in her shaggy fertility, handfuls fall, I slap handfuls back. She has risen off her sagging bed in my form, which is protean. I am cool with exterior cunt; I am night-laden with womb. I am petal-soft and glossy as melted chocolate. My clothes drag like brocades, my limbs slide luxuriously in their oiled tubes. The bosom of my shirt is heavy with breasts swollen with black milk among the bewitched butters.

Where is my white lover? He was here, and we stood in front of each other, delaying our moment of contact, and he raised his arms to embrace me, and he vanished. I rose to meet him, but he was gone. I smell of tar and sunlight; where is he? I will enjoy the sun-light while I can. Soon he will return, but I shall be sleeping, gone into the sleeping tides. It is the only way he can return. He will sponge himself down with the wet mosses. He will erase me with the small clear wavelets advancing over my picture. He will rinse my black blood off in his bathroom; I will fade like a shadow in his shower of bright water.

I stand in the shower-booth under the knives of water that are skinning me, skinning her, cleaning me; the last traces of her dwindle and leave. A few half-rotted leaves stick in the drain. My skin glows with vitality. It is my new skin; the old has peeled away. I step out of my sodden clothes, I towel myself, I sit down at my table and my journal. I write an account of how I have visited my left-hand bride in the other world. This is my dowry: this glow like noonday in my skin. Now I would be ready for a right-hand bride; would that it were Madame.

Thus I return again and again to this dance of Antaeus, to the uncreated. Others possess other renewals. This is my dance, clothed in opulence of golden mud. I know the people here. Their dances are — saner, are they not? The majority will recoil from a dance like mine. I cannot understand that they should. It would renew them. Yet I cannot say that all is well. Why can I not know myself and my left-hand bride at the same time? She fades like the night in order that I may return. It is as if a mother died afresh each time her child called for her in the night, and rose from her death only when the child was sleeping again.

There are so many dances. Now the time approaches when Daniel will bring all the people out to dance and all the dances will be joined into one. Will I perform my dance among all the others, will my dance fuse with the dance of the world?

That time has arrived! The trumpets are blowing. Six men

marching in Sunday black wind the small silver trumpets through the village streets. Six women in village white bow the small dark violins. The music wakes me in the tavern bed. My dancing clothes have been dried and ironed for me and hung up without comment. I dress scrupulously. My willow-wand leans in a corner; I take it in my hand and clatter down the wooden stairs. Outside a Flora Dance plays from loudspeakers on poles that line the street. People are dancing in procession up the winding path that leads to the dancing-ground on the hill. Save for the orchestra, they are dressed in skins and hides. The sun shines. My skin glows. The Flora Dance plays from all the flying beaks of the innumerable birds.

How can I dance my desire on the hard earth of this ground? My left-hand bride — how old her soul must be — will not rise from dry earth! Sweat in the dance will not give her life; only the tide. The music ceases as we attain the plateau. Music played to assemble the people; they must dance to the sound of their own flesh chafing the earth and their breathing. There is a lady presenter in skins and a veil of hide; is this Madame? She gives her people their turn to dance with the touch of a green bough.

All are masked with ragged veils of hide. I am the only naked face here. I can recognise dwarf Daniel as he dances his subject: the tearing and devouring of flesh. Madame (is it she?) selects his partners to dance for him the dismemberment he desires. He dances his selection of the great knives and the cleavers, he mimes the stalking of his victim, who dances her disbelief as he slashes and severs her limbs and she falls from her legs. Her life pumps into the ground, the soaking blood mimed by wriggling fingers. Daniel squats in his hides watching the five headless carcasses jerk and thrash in the sunlight, and licks blood from the pieces. But there is no blood, no victims. The sweat of the dancers smokes in the air; there is only the smell of leather and sweat.

Now three men are chosen to dance the filling of gas-chambers and the fuelling of ovens with this entire company. I cry out as I understand; the women stretch up to the sky as they convulse in the invisible shower-stalls; the lady stands aside. My cry is the only sound, but as I wear no mask I remain unseen.

Now I watch a group dance the knocking together of a ship of great size from the bodies of other dancers, and the spreading of its sails, and from this ship they exclude a certain number. Animals of certain kinds are admitted dancing two by two; the remainder dance the great waves folding in, and the excluded people and animals dance drowning, their bodies drifting down into the waters, their eyes bulging, their fingertips again stretched out to the light as they sink. It was the lady presenter who chose the ones for the boat and those for the drowning. Though I am on the fringes of the dance and I wait with my face bare for the lady to choose me, even for the drowning, she passes me by. With her green bough she confirms the others in their courses or turns them aside. When the billows come curling and cresting she rises above them like the moon itself.

Now I watch the Banshee-woman dancing the laundering of ghosts. How she pummels them again and again on hard boulders in the rushing stream. The lady selects all in turn except the unmasked one to enter the banshee-water to be pummelled empty of guts like suits of their own skin. Then the banshee mimes the swelling of her belly and the knitting of children together in the womb with the bone needles of her long nails. The waiting spirits pass one by one in turn through her spread-out legs, hauling their great life-support hoses behind them, which the crone nips off in her teeth.

Now the lady begins her dance. It must be the chief dance, since the others have been obedient to her touch and the language of her wand. At first she dances alone; the men form a corridor and watch her spin among them. Then they take paces back, and it is a circle of all the men. Dancing clockwise, the lady touches each man with her bough, and as she does so, the man dances certain steps to demonstrate his quality. She chooses one who can bound and leap; he bounds with legs wide into the centre with her. He shall dance sun and stag. I have not been called upon to demonstrate any quality.

There is a sigh of joy from all the company. There is a dance of riding and intercourse; the couple dance on their heels to indicate the possession of hooves. There is stamping and drumming, charging and chasing; there is rolling, and there is slow beating of the feet of all the company until the ground trembles as with waves of the sea. There is a dance of double serpent in which the lady and the lord lead all the others except the barefaced one in a winding serpentine course with two centres between which all the dancers twine, the lady at one, the lord at the other, who seek each other's glance over the heads of their company. I who have not been chosen cower in case I intercept the glance of one or the other, in case I do not intercept the glance. Body-sounds and breathing are the only music.

Now the procession reforms and to the sound of trumpets and violins the villagers descend to their houses. None of them looks at me. Not even the great black man who has danced sun.

When I have understood that they wish to pass me by, I fall in at the tail of the procession winding down the dancing-hill. We dance a slow step in triple time to the sound of strings, trumpets and a little drum. My feet drag along the path, but soon the music restores my spirits and I dance like the others, but like a dead person, unseen, dancing. I expect all to disperse each to his home at the village square, and I turn towards the Falling Leaf Tavern, but my arms are gripped like an arrest! The two hinder dancers, with serious mouths under their visors of skin, force me to stay. The procession forms again, but it has turned and I and my captors are at the head of it. Now to the sound of music we dance out of the village towards the tidal inlet. I cannot see the lady; is this reversal with her permission? As we approach the mud-flats the musicians fail silent again, and the only sound is the chafing of skin across earth.

We reach the flats where the walls and dykes are under construction to reclaim the land. The tides have renewed my dancing-floor, which was a marsh like a destroyed bed bearing the imprints of our bodies; it is glossy and smooth as black glass in which the sunset is reddening. The two hinder dancers have set me on the turfy bank, they have released me and have stood back. All wait silently, and I understand that I am to perform my dance for everyone. My fear leaves me. I take my willow-wand in my right hand and lean over the mud and trace the first features of my left-hand beloved, her crescent brows. I bound off the bank and landing perfectly begin to stamp and scoop the eyes. With lively steps I leap and prance, scribe and step and scoop until I stand again in the feet of my completed figure, facing out to sea. Because the sun is now in the west, it is behind me. I turn with a leap to face the red sun, plucking my feet out and stamping them down. I see the throng watching me from the bank, like black cut-out figures against the sky.

One steps out from among them, into the disc of the red sun. She is a woman of shadow in black bodice and long skirt sweeping and a tall headdress like a bride. Suddenly this silhouetted figure leaps out of the sun into the mud and stands knee-deep in the waist of my figure, her skirt spreading over the earth. I approach her and see that it is the lady, and now my eyes are not dazzled I see that she is dressed in white, and veiled. We face each other across the deep trench of the cunt. She crouches and throws herself forward into the birth-place. She rolls, lapping herself in the black plasm. I throw myself forward and we lie like twins embracing in the womb of richness.

We lie there as the mud receives us and begins to cover our heads. We turn until we are facing the east, and pull ourselves on our bellies out of the thighs of the figure. She stands in the shallows and stretches arms and legs out like a black star; I lie at her feet like the blacker shadow of a shadow.

But we are neither of us shadows! Both lovers are present, together, at the same time. So I caper with my left-hand bride in the great mud. We dance earth and water and the yeasty air and the reddening fire of the sun, which strikes smoky azures, mauves, crimsons, velvety blacks and vermilions from the watery mud. She holds a handful out to me and within the colours I see the detail, the stems and shards of wood unravelling like tapestry; the sandy grains, each one giving the sun back out of itself like a lamp; the leaves like fragments of the caparisons of beasts; discarded skin of caddis like minute crooked hose jewelled like a king's boots with tiny sand; purple berry-skins.

Then the handful goes slap on my head and in a slow-motion dance like clowns assaulting each other in the great bilberry-pie circus-scene we interchange harmless insults by scooping and plastering. Then we dance seamless statuary with our sweet-sour skins joined. She lays me down and rolls me like a seed in the blue-black earth; she pulls me out into the sunlight like a germinating oak, birth-wet and plastered with my foliage. Then we are serpents in the mud, wriggling out of our glistening skins and back into them again. Then we are hulks in the old docks slowly consuming among the tides of rust. Then we are headless, handless joints of meat basting in our rich greases in the red oven. And we are bread rising because of the yeast in us. We fashion new and surprising organs out of our plentiful clay and wear them proudly for a while and then dash them away. She grows a mud-face baby with a skeleton of twigs and rushes under her flounces; and I suckle our tar-baby with the purple milk out of my ruined shirt. Now we bury our baby and stamp it down because we want to be alone; its body dissolves; we are careless because there are many such babies where that one came from. I bury my lady and she buries me and we are mute mounds mourning, that break open after a decent interval just like the resurrection. Then we caper again and make love in the queasy bed, with the whole queasy bed under the eyes of the onlookers, for it is our dance, and the ripples of our embraces reach the farthest shore.

The silent watchers on the bank raise their black trumpets to their lips and signal the end of our dance. My lady rises from the embrace and I rise and our mud-laden clothes have fallen away with our antics and remain unravelling in the mud. We dance naked towards the crisp foam that dances towards us from the east as the tide rises. My berry-skinned lady enters the white foam. I enter the white throats of the foam formed like lilies and singing like trumpets. We plunge head over heels in the blinding foam.

I run gasping from the tide. The two foremost dancers advance to meet me, and to the sound of music they clasp a garment about me to warm my body. I turn towards the waves from which my lady should rise from the sea to join me. But the sea is empty and the foam crisps gently in hollow waves.

The people draw me shivering away from the sea and its empty foam.

This lady has ended in the sea, just like the lady I made for myself. This dance is no better than the other! The dancers dry my tears at the edge of the foam and urge me with many gestures to join in their dance. But why should I dance among those who are no more than bloody foam and mud dancing on bones! But I do so dance, and as I dance lover-less, the warmth of the dance causes me to forget. Soon I am bounding and leaping, stamping, passing under arches of arms, encountering new partners and evading old ones, dancing ferociously with the men, who dance among ourselves before we divide and share out the women, whom we lose to others in the new rejoinings.

As chance would have it I meet up again and again with a certain lady, whose carriage and figure remind me of the lady I lost. I cannot tell who she is because of her visor of skin, but at last the dance arrives in which we unmask. I welcome this dance because it is the dance of which I have always been a member, having prepared myself by carrying no face but my own. Now I see as I have been seen. I dance in partnership with this certain lady, whose face is visible for the first time, whoever she may be. The dance breaks up. Many are paired, as we are. We wend our way to the tavern door. We climb the wooden stairs, we bathe, we sleep together in the great bed, we wake unveiled to each other's bodies. Now we are dressing each other. I button her blouse gently up to her throat so that the points of the collar make a little A. I pass her pendant engraved with the A and the V inside the o over her fine dark hair. She buttons my shirt but leaves the neck open so that my throat is bare in a V. Her mask of skin lies empty on the bedside table. She says to me: 'You have passed your threshold awake, at last.'

* * * * *

'She wants to get a child from a psychic man.' Sir Geoffrey handed me another of his scripts written in big script fizzy as a startled cat's tail.

'That is her plot,' he said, waving his hand round at the day-room of the Institute, 'the reason for all this.' He hummed reflectively, stroking the tightly coiled black hair on his bare chest.

'We were chosen,' I said. I still had my own plot to marry her.

'Many were called. I wonder whether I could be called psychic.' I looked sideways at him. If Madame wanted a *black* man. . .

'Yes, I wonder if I'm psychic.' He frowned. 'Is it psychic to be able to turn one's night-soil into conscious language?' He bared his great grin, swiftly closed his lips again and was serious. I made no answer. 'We've all been exposed to apparently psychic phenomena. I think that's to see whether such events, simulated or not, will stimulate the like in ourselves!'

'I was raped by a spirit!' I had told Sir Geoffrey about this in strictest confidence.

'Raped or pleasured? That could be a test. They say Love conquers all.'

In a way, I had been repeatedly raped by a spirit all my adult life, so I knew what I was talking about.

Ever since I had been a man it had pulled me into what Freud recoiled from and called 'the tide of black mud of the occult'. Now I supposed the whole Peninsula knew, including Madame. The important question was whether my madness was interesting enough to make her laugh, and marry me. I looked at Geoffrey. He had been born a good colour. My black washed off. Geoffrey would need to go elsewhere in Cornwall for such a dance, to bathe in the blinding white mud of the china-clay pits.

'I think the spirit pleasured all of you simultaneously in that seance.' I had come to that conclusion myself. 'Except for me, but then, I was dozing. As you know, the script that resulted was an erotic poem. These were certainly no impotent ghosts. Perhaps the post-mortem genius of an extraordinary person; maybe even David Dimitrios. That would be natural, even though it was supernatural . . .'

'No, not impotent,' I muttered.

'Or,' and Geoffrey frowned a little, 'even a pre-vitam; somebody trying to get born. Fertile, then; is that how Madame will choose?'

* * * * *

THE PREGNANT SPIRITUALIST

By mere breathing, she sees her own shape,
The solemn tranquillity of her naked life
Under her clothes, the day-long caress;

By careful breathing, a luminous womb-ghost beneath,
The tranquil solemnity of its shrimpy shape.
The tie of each sitter like a rope

Rolling the skull, their understanding
Being washed in blackness, she is
Cleaning their heads with night,

In her chant, her moaning chant;
They nod their heads and take it,
All of them, in their circle, the sitters,

Joining their facilitating hands.
She has a baby in her womb that sways in its bonds;
In trance, that baby is, beating through its veils,

And she tells herself this child is of such virtue
'I am made a prophetess. Accordingly I speak
Out of the womb to these adventurers.'

The room is psychic, the whole space answering;
The draperies at the windows fall in grimaces,
Straining to speak, the great seamed faces;

The atmosphere, like birth-water, is living currents
Tapping out her heartbeat, and there slowly swims
The disc of the luminous tambourine,

Taps out that same shiver to which there floats
And forms above their rocking heads an ectoplasm
Like a foetus in its robes,

Or like a lily unfolding, and from the draperies
Steps out a spirit naked as pips, with
A few wisps caught up for modesty,

Singing as with the sound of silver bells
And tambourines. Madame knows
She magnifies by these seances,

This is the adult image of her child
As she might be, and prays
She will one day meet her so

In their afterlife together; but now
She is the hovering centre of their circle, they may ask
Their questions, and to one she is

The dead wife returning, in her lace; to another
The spirit who rapes him; and another
Sees her dressed in cauls for a wedding,

Belled in white as for a wedding: 'But for me,
She is simply my future,
Growing in me and talking round this table.'

'It's certainly a theory,' I said, passing back his paper and getting out my tobacco-pouch.

* * * * *

I was passing the refectory, and happened to glance through the swing-doors. The kitchen staff was being harangued by a tall figure in a hat with a broad brim from which a white beekeeper's veil fell to merge with the long-skirted pale dress. I pushed one door ajar and heard that well-remembered voice of the relaxation-tape. As I pushed through, the figure turned and left.

I hurried past the staff busy laying the tables, towards the kitchen. It was, however, empty, with its broad bench-tops, its great range, and the shining copper pans. I looked into the scullery but that exit was locked, with the key on the inside. As I returned up the stone step into the kitchen I saw under a staircase a heavy wooden door standing open. Inside were steps winding downwards. A bright light shone on the wall below, where the stairs turned. I descended a few steps and called out 'Hello! Is there anybody there?' The only answer was an angry spurt of noise that sounded as if a wasp or bee had got caught down there. It was followed by a peal of silvery laughter. Much intrigued, I went down further, and turned the corner of the winding stair.

I was astonished to find myself in a lavishly furnished room. It opened out through an arch to the right indicating that this was only the first apartment of an extensive cellarage. The walls were rather sombrely coloured in whirling patterns of amber and black. Opposite hung a tapestry showing a classical landscape with a goddess suckling her baby among hives. Along the stair were hung a number of framed medals and diplomas having to do with beekeeping. Everywhere among the amber and black, and shining out in the brightness of the light, was the flash of gold; the gold medals, the gilt lettering of the prize-certificates and diplomas; a gold-framed mirror to the left; large bees with outstretched veiny wings done in gold and pinned to the wall in a flight like china ducks; on a little table by an armchair a gold comb and brush and a gold-mounted mirror; in the armchair a figure whose veil was now secured at the crown by a gold coronet or cincture, and dark eyes looking at me through the veil. She reached up and took off the circlet, then the veil. It was a woman I had never seen before. The angry insect sound came once again.

Glad of a diversion, I said, 'Just a minute. There's a bee or wasp caught in here. I'll get rid of it for you.' The woman showed her teeth in a smile. 'Why,' I said, 'it's you. You're doing it!' She was making the sound between her meeting teeth.

'That was my Sunday joke. I loved to do that in church when I was a girl. To upset God's stuffy Sunday. We had the pew by the hollow pillar. It made a good whispering gallery or echo-chamber. I'd do the humming, a little at first, here and there during the sermon, then the dive-bombing, and everybody would duck. A bee in church is a terrifying thing. Once in, how do you get it out? Is it a wasp, a hornet? People start to see it everywhere. Is it that burr on a skirt, that blob of candle-wax on a vestment? We are no match for fast angry insects.' She did the bee-impression again, and the ventriloquism was so accomplished that I really did seem to see the fast-moving little blur circling the room. 'Only my father took no notice. He knew what it was.'

'Was his name David Dimitrios?'

'Wouldn't you like to know! I'm Julia. You think I'm Madame.'

'Aren't you?'

'I could be. How will you find out?'

'Somehow.'

'Then you'll try and propose to me, like all the others.'

I found I was blushing.

'I'm very anxious to meet Madame, and if you are she, then I'm overjoyed.'

'If I were Madame, I wouldn't let on. Not before we had got to know each other. You see, she is very rich. She has unscrupulous suitors. Female staff have instructions not to admit they are not Madame. This is not my admission that I am not she.'

'You're teasing.'

'Of course.'

'When did you last see Madame, if you're not Madame?'

'Oh, not for ages.' She picks up the hand-mirror. 'Or just now. She could be anywhere.'

'You know, I find you impossibly attractive.'

'Even though I dress like a ghost?'

'Oh, very much so. That was why I followed you.'

'I thought it was Madame you were after.'

'I don't care if you are Madame or not. I simply want to know you better.'

'That's more like it! It could be the point at which I'm allowed to admit that I'm not Madame.'

'The admission would be a perfect disguise for the real Madame.'

'Why must you always be talking about that woman!' She tossed her head, got up and glided towards me. She took my hand.

'You must meet my friends,' she said, and drew the bee-fobbed curtain at the archway. I became aware of the distant crying of a baby. 'Do you really want to know where Madame is?'

'I very badly want to meet her. So far I've only heard her speaking. The first time was on a tape. That was like a ghost made of rust-marks on plastic. I followed it here.'

'I'm not a ghost. Touch me.'

'Ah no, you're not a ghost.'

'Will you still be interested if I'm not a spirit?'

'You're exceedingly spirited.'

'Spirited! How horsy . . . we all have a little of Madame in us in this place. Her spirit. Her flesh.' I thought of possible lesbian bee-rituals between worker bees, the sterile females. It would ruin the hive! I had heard that the lesbian experience surpasses by far the heterosexual encounter. Since both partners are naturally capable of multi-orgasms, there is no upper limit to the altitude of their wedding flights. This made me cautious.

'You speak as though Madame were a sacrament.'

'We would take honey as a sacrament, honey and comb, blood of the sun, flesh of the flowers, blood and flesh of the hives.

'Do you still take that communion?'

'We have fallen rather behind since . . .'

'Since Madame went?'

'Why do you keep hinting that she's gone? I tell you that she's here!'

'You asked me whether I really wanted to know where she is!'

'It's a secret.'

'I promise not to tell.'

'You must take an oath.'

We had passed through a number of rooms, all as opulently furnished, and with variants of the same tapestry in each, but with different trees in flower and different weather, but the same hives in each, and the same goddess suckling her growing child. In the fifth room were half a dozen whitish translucent cradles in a substance like wax. There were babies in the cradles.

'Heavy-duty polythene,' she tucked one of the children in more securely; 'we were each given two when we were initiated as Queens. David always expected twins. Which is what he got.'

'All of you? Are there other women here? Are these the children of Dr Dimitrios?'

'Each child is his daughter, and his grand-daughter too. Riddle me this.'

'You are Madame's sisters.'

'The grandmother-mothers of our daughter-grand-daughters.' She must be making this up, I thought. She is trying to hypnotise me by overloading my circuits.

'Then the spirit of Madame is one that you share through sisterhood and fatherhood.'

'Why must it be called her spirit! We all have it! David our father had twins twice. It was his magic. Then we twins had magic twins by David our husband.'

'Then one of you must be Madame's identical twin-sister. Why are there only six children here? Where are Madame's twins?'

'You will meet all of us soon.'

'But you're not screwed-up, are you? I mean, with that

complicated inheritance (if true, and I haven't worked out all the relationships yet, but I wouldn't be surprised to hear that somebody, probably Madame, was her own mother), I'd have thought that you'd all be pretty screwed up. I haven't met your sisters yet, or so far as I know I haven't, but since you're running an Institute for unscrewing people, you can't be screwed up yourselves. Can you?'

'David claimed to be the child of such a union. His argument was that the more mixed-up the parentage was, the less the offspring was exclusively that parent's property, especially when the parent had several roles in one, as aunt-mother, or father-grandfather. It promoted, he thought, the "family romance".'

'I would have thought it made it worse. Everywhere you looked there'd be the same father; if you wanted your mummy you'd get grannie as well!'

'It was the method of the Pharaohs. David also liked to introduce competing sperm. He thought the mother of his magical children should make love to several men, and the conception would be a virile composite, with the best strains winning. Twins were always the result of such a congrex, as he called it, in David's community. Twins like these children . . .'

'Apparently David released powers he couldn't control.'

'Yes, alas, so many died in the explosion.'

'Then hold on. That bomb exploded years ago. If David was their father, they'd be toddlers at least by now. You're having me on!'

'David believed that if intercourse took place in the presence of a fresh or embalmed corpse, then the spirit of the dead man that lingered about his mortal remains would enter into the child. The conception of these children was facilitated by many different sperms.' I thought of the female staff slipping under cover of the dark into our seances. 'Yet poor dead David also entered us in the flesh. He is here with us, as Madame is, and has always been . . .'

There was a little curtain in the wall I had not noticed until by means of gold strings she slowly drew it open. With mounting horror I saw a panel of glass inset in the wall like an aquarium, and floating behind that panel as she switched a little light on, pieces of, pieces of . . .

I woke to find Julia stroking my forehead, and no sign of the babies or the cradles. I looked over at the little red bee-embroidered curtain which had concealed the — tank. To my relief it was closed. I felt as I had after I had been raped by the spirit. I had a splitting headache. Under her fingers I felt about two years old.

'You fainted, my dear.'

'All that about David — was it true?'

'All what?'

'You being a pair of twins.'

'Oh, that. You've been reading his sex magic book.'

'I didn't know he'd written one. What's behind that curtain?'

'A holy picture.'

'Show me.'

She drew the strings and behind the curtain in a gilt frame was a picture of three women veiled as beekeepers contemplating a golden hive of the classical conical kind called 'skips'.

'I think that thoughts have a habit of bursting into the brain when one has been in a place that teaches them invisibly. You're not David's daughter.'

'I told you, I must not admit that I am not she. It is part of the treatment.'

'The stress thus engendered certainly had its effect. Thank you for facilitating me.'

'Do you still want to know all about Madame?'

'Not if it has that effect on me. Yes, I do.'

'Here are the others. My friends.' I was aware of another woman, by the tapestry. At the same time, a third appeared in the arch to the other room. They were dressed alike, looked alike, so strikingly it was like seeing the same woman in two places at once. I began to feel dizzy again. Julia saw my expression. 'Don't worry! They really are twins. Meet Anne and Jennie.' She spoke to them. 'He is ready for us. Please make yourselves ready.' With a smile at me they left the room.

'You know too much and too little. If I show you a little more you will know enough to satisfy you, and that will stop you prying too much. At the same time nobody will believe what you know, so you'll not be tempted to spill the beans.'

'What sort of beans?'

'Oh, a secret about our religion. Almost the final secret. Watch.'

She swung a lever on the wall I thought was a bell-pull. Its shaft was surmounted by a particularly beautiful model in gold of a long-bodied queen bee. The room's tapestry of winter swung aside. Behind were great doors that looked as though they were made of gold, and these swung open also.

She saw the question and amazement in my eyes.

'They are gold. Madame is very rich. Gold is incorr-uptible.'

The doors glided like wings, without sound, only whispers of air. Behind was a further room, with steps leading up to an immense circular altar spread with an amber cloth, a canopy over it supported by twining pillars up which more golden queen bees soared in flight.

'It is a bed,' she said, and led me towards it. The doors were closing behind us. I noticed a small access door in the side wall.

'You wanted to know more about our religion. We are the inner guild. I want to teach you Madame's exercise.'

'You promised to tell me how to reach Madame.'

'No I did not! I promised to tell you where she was. How you reach her is your own affair. I have not yet administered the oath. The oath is the exercise. It would take you a lifetime to describe what the exercise teaches. It is not such as you would learn from the likes of Daniel. I have seen Dr David and Madame clothed in living robes of bees, bride and groom with a skin of glittering wings, humming skins that spoke words in their soft undervoices and which crawled in patterns of oracles like living tattoos.'

'The bees spoke!'

'Like this, lover, like this.'

'Are there bees here? There is a hum that is growing in volume. It continues while you speak. I feel it and hear it. Your skin tastes sweet.'

'I am the swarm and the hive and the queen and the honey and the light and the sweetness. Bury yourself in me; I am the hive without stings. Dr David glided between the emptied hives, dark angel with his million wings. When our skins touched, the bees flowed between us and we were one.'

'Your skin is made of wings and velvet. It buzzes as I touch it, like a cool gong that you touch while it is still sounding.'

'I am like that everywhere, in every part of me, deep inside. Enter me, and you will know this with your root and centre, you will feel the hum with your deepest sense, and it will take you, lover. I am like that everywhere . . . everywhere . . .'

I touched her words as she spoke them; they formed themselves by touch in my skin. Then '. . . the Gate was opened to me, that in one Quarter of an Hour I saw and knew more than if I had been many years together at an University, at which I exceedingly admired . . .' This book that I am writing to tell you about the Institute lies in front of you because every detail, every tremor in it was implanted into my skin during that act. In writing this I am unravelling my skin, my skein. Not only this book, but all my acts to come. As if the skin had flowed, then set in a new pattern, my business to unfold that grain new-imprinted in me. Fiction and fact, what is before you now is the effort to express truthfully what I knew and felt in that moment. It was not now rape by the spirit; my innermost consented.

'That is our religion.' The soft voice came from a long way off, flying nearer. 'This is what we have all seen.'

'I believe you.'

'There is no death.'

'I believe you.'

'Only renewal, transmutation.'

'You. How could you, a mortal woman . . .'

'Us.'

'Us? Us? Who else is here!'

'Only the twins. Jennie and Anne.'

'The girls.'

I heard the girls laughing pleasantly, lightly; they hummed a little as if by habit, and with a certain air of satisfaction, and laughed again. I opened my eyes. Yes, I was in bed with the three women. I could see this very plainly in the round mirror fastened over our heads. The amber bedspread was gone; we were arranged on the black sheets like four white slices of a delectable wedding-cake.

'What is the matter?' said Julia; 'the flight is for us all, equally. Two bodies could not do all we have done. We shared you, and you shared us.'

'Shared!' The greatness of the experience made my disappointment all the more violent, though my feelings changed later. 'Share! This is not love — it is an orgy!'

'Men often feel a reaction after the vision.'

'Vision. Hallucination. Imposition. I thought it happened because you loved me.'

'So I do, yet I hardly know you. Jennie and Anne love you, though you have barely exchanged a word with them.'

'Four of us! Isn't there a less complicated way of seeing your truth?'

'I'm afraid not. Think — there are so many millions in the world. All are capable of it.'

'Oh yes — as long as you divide by four. So convenient, with over-population what it is. No wonder your Dr David came to a bad end.'

'This was not the reason that happened. What we did here is perfect health, perfect and abounding. You took the full charge of our longing.'

'Oh yes. Who was it yesterday? Daniel? Sir Geoffrey?'

'The black man comes to us often. Little Daniel is not that way inclined.'

'I'm not sure I blame him.'

'Will you believe me if I tell you that you were a good candidate in the initiation?'

'Candidate indeed! Are the examiners entirely satisfied? How nice!'

'You know the depths of what you saw. Or you will when you have had a chance to reflect.'

'I came looking for the explanation of a mystery.'

'We have shown you the mystery. There is no explanation of what happens when love is made. You have taken your oath by showing yourself capable of *seeing*. Your present bad temper makes no difference in the long run.'

'And you made a promise. This bed is too honied. I wanted a different kind of fact. I want to meet Madame.'

'Madame is here.'

'You keep on saying that. But I want to meet her face to face.' They laughed again at that. Anne and Jennie brought their single face close up to mine.

'How do you know that you haven't,' they said.

'That uncertainty again. Said to be part of the treatment. What's to prevent me telling all I know?'

'It will take longer than you think. Besides, as we told you, most people won't believe. Daniel will tell you what you want to know. He is the one who needs to tell. By listening you will be able to facilitate his confession.'

'Confession?'

'No more now. You must kiss us goodbye.'

I relented then, and kissed the three women tenderly in turn.

'Will love-making ever be like that again?'

'It is always like that, whether you know it or not.'

'What did they call you, the Queens, the women who gave initiation?'

'They called us sometimes *Suvasinis,* flowers, the sweet-smelling ones. But most often they called us Melissai . . .'

'Melissai. What does it mean?'

'It means "Honies".'

* * * * *

He was pleased because they were dressing in white clothes again. He got out his morris-gear, which had been cleaned and pressed for him without comment. The women wore simple white dresses, gathered like an academic gown across the shoulders, with big sleeves, but belted at the waist.

'Where are we going?' he asked.

'Into the woods.'

'By the little stream?'

He was thinking again of the black silt seams of woodland mud lying glittering in the semi-darkness like anthracite coal.

'No, the pine woods.'

'Ah. And the lamps.'

'We must take lamps. Will you help fill them?' There were six lamps: four were carbide using water and burning acetylene with its sheer white glare; the others were tilly-lamps with paraffin, having to be pumped up, and then glaring almost as white, but with a buttery-yellow tinge.

'Here, take yours.' The tallest of the three women was veiled like a beekeeper, but he recognised her voice. She handed him his lamp already lit. The little procession stepped out of the french windows and walked beating their wings of light and shadow across the lawn and up the little hill to the pine wood on its crest.

The night was dry and warm and the scent of the pines greeted and enfolded them. Passing through the slim straight stems gave the lamps a quick beat, like a strobe. They came to a clearing at the tip of the hill.

'Our custom is to stand with feet bare.' He kicked off his shoes and his feet enjoyed the cool pine-needles, strong and sliding one against the other, like pure glossy crystals.

'What are we doing here?'

The little man who was with them giggled and swung his lamp up to the speaker's face. A big dark moth like a splash of rich earth had fastened itself to the front of his shirt. Other moths were beginning to gather in beating globular clouds round his light.

'We're calling the piskies!'

The little folk! A shiver of superstitious energy bristled across his shoulders. The good folk — complimented thus because of their power: it was best that they were good, what life would be like if they were evil could not be endured. Was this some Celtic rite on the mump's tip? His skin felt disappointed that it could no longer, not tonight, look forward to some transformation, such as it sought in the mud. Or perhaps they might rend their garments and conduct their rite naked, wallowing in the lamplit air, sacrificing their polite outer husk to the good folk. Rags and half-nakedness were quite stimulating.

'How do I call them?'

'You have to stand as you are, and allow your lamp to swing in the rhythm which Madame will start up.'

A speckled moth with big head and golden eyes clambered like an epaulette on to the dwarf's shoulder. Madame's bright globe began to swing and the others followed her timing. Folds of shadow leapt out of the creases of their garments and as quickly withdrew. He thought that from outside the little wood, from down below, they must look like a single flickering lantern made of the hill's top, rowing the air with its beams; or like some being beating its wings there. Madame slowed the beat by paying out the cord fastened to the handle of her lamp, which lengthened its swing. So did the others. The beat of the lights was now almost hypnotic.

A big moth blundered into his eye. The air began to be full of the swimming flecks and blobs. Moths fell back singed from the bright globe of his lamp and twitched on the pine-needles. One became stuck in its frying substance to the glass. He stopped swinging and tried to brush the poor creature on to the cool ground.

'Keep the rhythm there! Keep the rhythm!' called out dwarf Daniel's imperious voice.

It was difficult to keep the rhythm. As the air filled up with moths of all colours and sizes one's head wanted to jerk from side to side to avoid them, weaving one's head like a boxer Gulliver among a mob of aeronautic Lilliputians. One had to breathe strictly through the nose, and keep the mouth sealed shut, and use one's free hand to brush the winged beings away from nostrils and eyes. One could not do anything about the hair. They must just roam there; it was so easy with even the lightest touch to pulp any fat-bodied moth that had got entangled there.

Suddenly the air was clear. He looked down at himself and saw that his white garments were alive with a skin of wings. Because of the lamps, the moths had been attracted to the glaring white that beat in rhythms like their own wings. Once the right rhythm had been found, they preferred the clothes rather than the darker flesh, glowing warm though it was, of faces and hands and throats. The garments had become a tawny ermine fleece, or like a fell, a speckled hide, a fox-fell that had grizzled silver. The spotted, the golden streaked wings, the eider-light, the black-helmeted, the skull-tabarded, the silver-and-lime of the striped hawk, the paisley of the oleander, and many many more, they were all on him; the imagined faint plucking of the infinitesimal horny claws, and a smell, very faint but equally definite yet unimagined, a sweetness like a minute purring, rose from his clothes; and underneath his skin prickled in a pattern that was delicate and feathering, quite unlike the great muddy hippopotamus river-kiss he had enjoyed with Madame in the estuary. Quite unlike. The veiled woman in the beating rhythm was now total moth, like a long fur coat and hat, and hood, and fluttering fur mask.

'Dowse your lamps!' said Daniel. Darkness shut down in sections; the individual lamps stopped swinging, and went out. Yet it was not quite dark, as he could see still on his body faint phosphorescences, and there was a tiny scratching heard, a little like distant radio static. He closed his eyes and saw painted on his eyelids, stretching out wide from between his brows, a great moth with a tigerish body and serene silver-beaked mask, gently beating its wings in a curious and uncanny after-rhythm. He felt sweetness like a wet dream and faintness as well. Was this another sexual materialisation? The markings on the underside of the wings flowed together like syrup dissolving in water and formed into Madame's face, bending forward to kiss. As the lips touched, his thoughts disappeared like a lamp dowsed.

He woke being carried downhill in a scent of pine.

'Please let me go.'

His legs struggled weakly; they were released. He took a few tottering steps, held by the armpits.

Daniel, standing in front of him with arms akimbo, like Henry VIII in spotless white, winked broadly. They were at the edge of the lawn, and a full moon had risen.

'Did you make your lucky wish to the piskies?' He leered. Yet was it a leer? He seemed to be able to see it two ways. In one way it was the strong and happy smile of an initiate.

'A moth kissed me. Should I have wished?'

'You must have got your wish without asking. A kiss and a swoon! Marvellous!' It was not a leer. It was happiness for a friend.

'A moth. A psyche. A piskie,' said Daniel.

'It had Madame's face.' This was whispered.

'Did it now,' said Daniel. 'How would you know? Well, you must have seen her at some time or another,' and courteously offered their new dreamer his arm. No, it was certainly not a leer. It was Madame's smile, after the kiss.

* * * * *

The waking thoughts of Madame. As many fish in the sea. The great grey salt moth, beating its tides. The dance of Jack-a-Dandy beating his wife with a gold stick, his water-wife, who veils herself in scented clouds. I wonder at the flowering clouds, they smell so sweet. Ah, a sudden stab of swallow-flight under the trees by the river; how ochre my footsteps in this clay, they shine.

Jack dancing on the water, leaving his footsteps to shine for a second: 'Oh sun, thou hast lodged dancing.' 'The great one crossed in the cabin, capped in the ark,' the spirit who is taller than his box, the houseboat that Jack built, the birth-place. A terrible child-bed, 'the belching whale/And humming water must o'erwhelm thy corpse,' little Jack, little Jake, Jacqueline's son, little sailor, called up out of the sea.

In the early morning twilight the ships are nests of blaze gliding towards the quays, or like oil-scented lilies of light wide open. Girls in pneumonia blouses line the quays, waving white lacy handkerchiefs. In front of the ships as in the front of the blouses, there are crisp ruffles where the prow cleaves. There is frost in the shadows like spirit photographs. The iron ship docks, ringing like a bell. As the first light glides into the town the old stone looks sweet and yellow as honeycomb. The holds of the ships are brimming with the little silver engines like silver pocket-pencils. They beat and leap; the greater engines are lulled from whirling in their golden oil as the ships draw in. The fisher embryos float in the pneumonia women with their foaming cleavage, little engines beating in their soothing oil, land-sailors breathing brine. And on the other hand are the salty fishermen bringing home the copious sea-sperm in silver milt-motes, finned notes to be tinned chords chiming slippery in their golden oil. There are spirits everywhere, spirit photographs. The air photographs the great sun humming in the sky, and everywhere it leaves its tracks, which are hives of bees; the sea snaps the moon and makes swimming milt, silvery sea-bees; and the women photograph the manly boats cleaving the sea, and their inner waters photograph the men, whose solid photographs are now growing within them, double exposure. The great spirit passes overhead wrapped in raining clouds and the early-morning scene creates itself by holography. The holds are full of elastic silver clockwork; and the dead who have descended through the rivers to the seas have ascended again by their work and become a fishy liquid trawled full of souls kept in the balls of potent fishermen for the briny women. The living and the dead greet the blouses ruffled like the waves where they have launched their prows, a human milt like oily nitro-glycerine that explodes slowly for ten sidereal moon-months. The old folk rock in their chairs like husks in a web, their houses full of wrinkles, and the fishermen swagger past their windows arm in arm with their shivering women, their pockets jingling full of silver.

Once I treasured a postcard of the Virgin Mary holding her hand cupped to a candle to stop it guttering. The light shone through the flesh of the Mother of God, the candle beating its wings in the dark hut. Jesus the fish, with ever-open eye, witness of the flood, his thin bones picked out in the coalfossil, shining in its black bed of the marshes crystallised by the hard aeons, body-print that is one of millions all the same, just the mark of his unmade bed, the print of his body left, and he went out that morning and died, poor child; the iron hulls ringing like cathedral bells, cathedral shining with its lamps of fish-oil through the slim pillars and the moths flocking. The priest wears black because he has mastered his shadow.

The crane glides on its rails with iron plates in its jaws towards the ruined tanker. It shines in the dawn like a celebrant serving iron. All the faces that swim along, the bodies just this side of water, a little fibrous wick at which the warm life sucks and flickers, their wickerwork bones, the fish that swim in their hordes and swarms, silver bees of the ocean, the faces shouting and weeping, and the tears never showing in all that brine, in a world of brine; as though we should never be able to weep anything more substantial than breath; their desolate faces and thin lips, their downdrawn mouths, their bones of thin horn, their lanthorn faces almost transparent with the drowned watery sunbeams shining through and picking out their cobwebby skeletons in which they are caught, the brain sitting on top like a fat spider with two humps; their shapes of tears streaming through the bitter water, each individually plated with silver and most minutely inscribed with scales, such herds and flocks mumbling the water, such orchards on the current-boughs, wafter wafer-thin, their whole lives a mark on the water, a travelling sketch, water-sheep, water-wheat, dip your bucket in and there's your feast.

The fish in the wave leaps from the crest, like the spirit bounding from the nether world, water stripping itself of water; the mother regards her watery belly and longs for the baby to clamber out of her like putting off a suit of clothes, a cumbersome diving-suit; the lover strokes the lover long hour after hour, striving to reach through layered skin after skin, desiring the lover naked increasingly; I was in my fighting-gear, my slippery silk shirt, and my veil empty on the chair; I had put off my cumbersome suit. He left silver hand-prints over all my skin, the shining lantern of man-oil; silver is the female metal because it corrodes and tarnishes easily, yet easily shines up to mirroring splendour. He came to me like a shadow of himself, in which the substance shone. The shadows have coupled. The man I have for husband must have mastered his shadow, in which until then I stand, veiled like the black frost.

* * * * *

The nurse I knew as Cecilia answered the door.

'Daniel's ill, I'm afraid.'

I remembered her as the nurse at Xavier's table, grumbling through a faceful of sliding custard. It had been her job to endure his enormous wet kisses of flung food. It was necessary to maintain the humorous atmosphere. Without this Xavier would plummet into desperation.

'Can't he see anybody?'

'No, I'm afraid he can't. As you'd understand if you could see him. He has hives. His eyelids are so swollen that he can't see out of them.'

'Is it infectious?'

'No. We think it was brought on by a bee-sting. He can hardly endure the warmth of another human body in the same room, the skin is so sensitive. We've just rung up the hypnotist.'

'I thought there was a hypnotist on the staff. The brochure says there is.'

'There is. It's Daniel. So we've had to send out. Hypnotism is the only answer. The effect is almost miraculous.'

I thought of what the girls in the cellar had told me. Daniel had something to confess. What was hypnotism after all but relaxation and credulity?

'I am a qualified hypnotist.' It was said on an impulse. I would regard the lie as part of my courtship.

'What a blessing! We know that the oedema will reach his lungs and drown him if something isn't done quickly.' Drowned in one's own body-fluids – ugh!

'Who shall I say you are?' I ignored that one, and started walking through the door. She gave way, good-humouredly.

As soon as I got into the flat I felt the atmosphere, like thunder, like undischarged clouds.

'Is your job very difficult?' I asked the nurse.

'Sometimes it is, sir. Mr Daniels can be an exceptionally awkward patient. He creates an atmosphere round him you could cut with a knife.'

I noticed in the living-room one of those big gilt mirrors of the kind I had already seen in the cellar. This one, however, had a crack in it like black lightning striking downwards from top left to bottom right.

'The mirror — what a shame!'

'It's the humming. His prayers. He wanders from room to room vibrating his prayers: you know the hum? This morning when he noticed the sting and realised an attack was coming on, he called me. I made him his lunch and brought it in — he had been humming ever since I arrived — and he was standing on a little stool in front of the big mirror. His red hair was bristling and his body was plump and tense and shiny-dark with the hives so that he looked like an angry bee, sir, and he was buzzing fit to bust. But it was the mirror that bust, with a crack like a gunshot. Mr Daniels just stood there, looking at his split image.'

I wasn't sure that this girl was all she seemed to be. I looked directly into her eyes and said, 'I think you should put a sheet over it.' Then, without changing my tone, 'Where is Madame?'

'He was calling for Madame, sir. But only to himself, like. How do you mean? Madame is upstairs. I saw her this morning.'

'Was she veiled?'

'Of course, sir.'

'Ah.'

'May I take you in to Mr. Daniels now?'

'Just a moment. Are you Madame?'

'I'm not allowed to admit that I'm not Madame, sir.'

'Take me in to Dan.'

The room was in semi-darkness. I lingered near the door, trying to get my eyes accustomed to the darkness. A groaning voice spoke from an armchair.

'Who is it? Is that the hypnotist?'

I peered into the gloom. I could just see something leaden in colour sprawled on the seat of the armchair. It was round like a football, like a bloated spider. There were arms and legs swollen like sausages in links and red hair and a little twiggy penis. There was a blind facelessness smooth except for grooves tightly pressed together where eyes and nostrils should have been, and a puckered pore for the mouth, through which the breathing hissed and the voice groaned. The cheeks were so swollen that the snub nose was almost invisible except as a faint ridge. Breath gasped and whistled through the puckered aperture, and something like a self-deprecating laugh briefly boomed there.

'You must please forgive my nudity. I cannot endure the touch of clothes. My skin scorches at the slightest heat, like a photographic film. Please come no closer. It is hives, an extreme form of nettle-rash, as though I had been rolling in them. I assure you I have not. As though I had been stung by the multitude of bees . . .'

The abrupt and dislocated syllable of laughter came again from that mouth. It looked more like an arsehole in a baby's bottom. Bumface. I realised it would make the same sounds whether it was laughing or sobbing. Perhaps this was an explanation for the devils of the Middle Ages, who had bee-stung faces like bottoms and bottoms like faces. If he started drowning in himself, would I have to give this monstrosity the kiss of life? Facilitation should go so far!

'I have begun the treatment myself, Doctor, that we agreed on in case of an emergency, and as you taught me with the post-hypnotic suggestion. It was an emergency, and I would not have been able to speak to you without this help. I know you chaps like to call it "the relaxation response" nowadays, but you and I know it's the same old magic, don't we Doctor? But I would prefer you not to use your passes or your whirling light today. I am so swollen, so tense with the pressure on my skin. Your voice from that distance will entirely suffice. Look, it is as you taught me; I count to ten and I am already asleep. 1 . . . 2 . . . 3 . . . 4 . . . Dr David and I had such exercises. I have learnt your method. 5 . . . 6 . . . 7. . . 8 . . .'

I was satisfied. Daniel was putting himself to sleep without my help, and would direct his own cure, without realising it. Meanwhile I would learn what I needed to know. Mutual self-interest. It was the essence of facilitation.

'9 . . . 10. I am asleep, Doctor, asleep and remembering.'

'You are asleep. Asleep and awake at once, and travelling deeper into yourself, into your past with each outbreath.'

My memory of the relaxation-tape in Madame's voice was still fresh in me. If I followed her technique I could not go far wrong.

'Deeper, and deeper.'

'Oh, this skin swollen and taut like an egg hatching my guilt. I hated her, hated her so deeply, and loved my master David. He made me feel tall in his presence!'

'Where is your master now?'

'Oooh,' the groan was heart-rending, 'torn to pieces by the explosion, by the riff-raff bombers. What a waste, oh the waste.'

'And where is Madame?'

I could not help asking the usual question. The result was startling. Dan arched his back and slid off the seat of the armchair. Once on the hearthrug he started bouncing about and whistling in agony, like a spider on a barbecue brick, or a saint on a griddle. It was as if every fibre of the long-haired rug was piercing him with its individual flame. I rushed over to him and picked him up. He felt like a big medicine-ball full of lukewarm water, and he screamed with a noise like a locomotive letting off steam all the while my hands held him. I put him back on the armchair and waved my hands over him.

'Sleep now,' I intoned, 'that was the angry threshold of your deepest sleep, the rapids in which you are cleansed and purged. You are over the threshold, this Niagara of confused dreams, over the tearing brink into calm water, safely. Now you are moving calmly, into safe water, into calm reflective water. Remember, and tell. Confession will ease your skin. Remember, where is Madame, the gifted one?'

Madame's technique had put me on the right lines. Daniel was deep in trance. One would have expected the pain to have woken him up, but no doubt it was an escape for him. Painful memory might be better than the physical torments of hives.

'Oh, I hated her so much, so much; the slim veiled one,

towering over me with her gifts and her tits. I loved my master more than anybody; my master loved her more than he loved me. I know he slept with her and the others to make his magical children. Wasn't I his magical stepson? Why couldn't he sleep with me? No, he said, quite kindly, he was not that way inclined. It was Madame who composed the miracles. I was the St Paul, the Petar, the talker, the poster of epistles. I was never initiate as she was. I could not endure the touch of bees, nor hazard their sting, for I should be as you see me now, swollen like a woman in labour. I curse the Mothers, the Mothers, for I am not one.'

The mouthhole was puckered still more and between the laboured words the breath was striking long notes of whistle on the rigid lips. The swollen tongue moved on its traverse between the puckering, sometimes like a heavy gun poking from a porthole, sometimes curved and pressing hard from inside like the crown of something trying to get born. I could hardly hear the next words, for the din that accompanied them.

'No blood, no glorious bitter red; only the golden honey, so heavy, so sweet. Not bloodstains I could wash, wash away; just that taste in my mouth spreading and staining the bones of my skull, that taste always in my head, so strong and sweet. Aagh. Aagh.' He shuddered and retched. A little green bile trickled over his immense cheeks. 'My murther like a feast . . . my murther.'

There popped into my mind for no conscious reason what he had told me about the great occasion of the sung Mass of the Beekeepers. He was shivering. There was a dove-grey wrapper, a coverlet of some silky kind on the floor. I drew it over him and he sighed with pleasure at its delicate touch. The skin had eased. We were making progress. What murder? I had often wondered whether any of us had anything to fear from any one of us. Had any inmate performed some masterpiece of negative facilitation that got him to the Institute? Like murder?

'Your murther, as you call it? But you are floating like a rubber ball bobbing in a calm reflective lake, and your recovery will form without distortion around you in the quicksilver water, and remembering will make you well. I take you back to that occasion, all the disciples gathered. Madame is there, and is the cantor, and you hate her, and your hate is quite natural, and it gives you mental energy, for you are the right-hand man of dear dead David; you have your inheritance for you are his interpreter, his authority. Go back to that time, let the scene in the great elliptical arena with the stage at the north form around you, calmly floating, untouched by all that happened, keenly seeing, as in the waters of your calm.' I had been into the great hall of the Institute but once, since its doors that led off from the refectory were usually sealed with great blobs of beeswax on golden cords knotted around the handles, each blob impressed with the sigil of a queen bee in flight. I had wandered in there once. The seals were gone, the doors ajar. It must have been opened for cleaning. It was all decorated with broad stripes of amber and black, and without lights it felt imprisoning, as though I were caught inside the long and vaulted empty body of a dead queen bee, the insides of which had been long hollowed out and eaten away. I touched the wall. It was done in a flock paper, that had the feel of velvet. In the middle, on a stand that looked like scaffolding, was a machine made of two globes joined together in a dumbbell-shape. Each globe was studded with innumerable lenses of various sizes. Then I looked up and saw that the ceiling was white, and that I was standing in a planetarium.

'Think back to that time, the great hall bright with the beeswax candles, down below, light upon light in hives of light, the orchestra assembled with its instruments of organic materials, of polished horn, shoulder-blade violins, harps of bone; the planetarium stars revolving like reflected hives of light above; the orchestra humming to tune up, and the congregation humming to their A also . . .'

'No, no — the stars are not to be turned on until the song begins! I gave the strictest instructions. Our Lady the Moon would appear in her full dress of light over the eastern horizon and cross over the hall, and the constellations would attend as the bees that issued from inside the shining hive of her!'

He continued without my prompting.

'One of the bees had stung me in the mouth that day. The pain made my many tasks as administrator of the occasion difficult; it was difficult to concentrate except by humming. Madame told me that it was a sign I was not to preach before the Mass. I was furious! I had not intended to; but it was plain she wanted to hold the stage as the sole cantor, the cunt. I forgot both pain and hatred when the music began. We thought we had known humming, but as the great bass hum of the congregation beat out, the orchestra added modulation upon modulation to this throb, changing it in innumerable ways as though the sound we made came from the big waves of a far-distant Atlantic storm spending itself on a coastline full of history and detail, which reflected back into the bay water the presence and patterns of its stones and homes until the whole coast was charged with changing and unfolding detail and pattern. This music hummed and buzzed in the ways we knew, but better than we had ever known; in their patterns and policies the bees were masters here below; that composer – he was an initiate of the heavens also, for as the great solo song arose so did the planetarium moon, attended with its swarms of stars, and the patterns of sound we made reflected the policies and patterns of the stars as the glad lights crossed the heavens. I knew we must play that cantata to our hives, and the hives would know their source and origin, and give us the taste of it in their honey, and their intelligence would tap it out on the skins of those who could endure the message. I know that Dr David had a scheme of genetic engineering: to get the best singers he would cross boys with bees, his messengers to every land; we wanted to drench the Queen with the fresh semen of little boys; and I must continue with his work; but now Madame was a part of that work, and I hated her no longer, under the projected moon and stars, in her amber and black and her long cape of wings, alone on the stage as the lights wheeled overhead, her naked face turned upwards to the constellations of visual song which she was answering with her own voice for us all, calling out to the gods.

'I knew there was a climax to the work, but I did not know its nature. It came when Madame shut her mouth firmly, and with a graceful gesture laid her hand with her finger extended over it, but the song went on, light, yet as if multiplied into many hundred thousand voices, the multiplication of the notes producing a buzzing that was far different from the crude bourdon that we had made or the accompaniment of the orchestra. It came, this chorus, from her whole body, it rose from the surface of her skin, as if every one of the many billion cells had found its note and was singing it in harmony with every other cell in the hive of her body, loud and clear and decisive. It was no trick, not mere art, it was our discipline raised to its uttermost. Then, ah . . .'

'Deeper and deeper, steadier and steadier . . .'

'. . . the chorus deepened and strengthened and a gladder sound entered it, so glorious, and it left her figure, this music, and swept about the hall, and all our heads followed it watching the invisible swarm wheeling in the air above our heads, and swooping and seeming to pass right through our bodies, making the hum with a zest, plunging deep into the foundations of the building, then up again, round, once, twice, thrice, and with added ecstasy on each circling, then without warning swooping through the north wall behind the stage, and silence fell, leaving Madame standing in the steadily moving lights, still and tall, with her still forefinger pressed to her lips, in the utter silence.

'I swear it was her soul flying. It was the next stage of our religion, perhaps of evolution itself. As Petar I began to formulate the phrases. To detach the non-material soul by making the body sing. To travel wherever and however one wished, in the form of an invisible choir of bees, maintaining the pattern by song like an unbuilt beehive or a cone of electromagnetic broadcast sweeping through the universe, a vortex of energy like a burning hollow star, returning to the stars from which everything we knew once came. Each initiate an angel of a million wings, a million eyes, each eye with a million facets beaming its patterned radiation. The meaning of what we had heard and seen sank in on us all slowly, while Madame's figure remained on the stage, and our applause beat on her like that Atlantic storm . . . ah . . .'

'Deeper and deeper. .

'And the applause raged for many minutes, then faltered as Madame remained motionless, still as a statue, finger hushed to lips, and we understood we must remain silent in order to witness the many-winged soul returning to take up its habitation in the hive that was our Mistress. She would return. And . . .'

'Deeper and deeper, it is all over, cannot hurt you now . . .'

'I fear it has only just begun . . . my heart was in that applause, and my love was in the silence following, but the silence lengthened, and I began to wonder as the minutes ticked by, and as I was the Petar, the shower, the spokesman, it was up to me to know best what to do, to bring the proceedings to their proper conclusion. So I left my seat in the front row, and I climbed the stage stairs towards that still, illuminated figure, long finger laid to her lips, my own arms held out for the first time towards this great Lady, my heart swollen with my feelings and love . . .'

'Nothing can hurt, all is calm, your vision is clear . . .'

'As I got close I saw that Madame's face glittered in the starlight. It was wet, with tears, I thought. Closer still, looking up at her face, I could see that her eyes were not closed, as I had believed, but were strangely clouded over. On tiptoe I looked into them, as they seemed to stare over my head into the distance. It was as though clear surfaces had crystallised. I touched her cheek with my finger. The tears were sticky. Without really meaning to, I put my finger to my lips, imitating her gesture, to my mouth. There was a superb sweetness on it, like a magnificent honey. It was such a surprise I scarcely knew what I was doing, but I swear there was love in my heart. I wanted her to speak, to reveal all she knew so that I would become as she was. I reached up again and touched the still finger that sealed her lips in the gesture of silence. Ah . . .'

'Deeper and stronger . .

'Ah me, it was as cold as wax. I could not believe it, and my hand was shaking as I gripped the finger lightly as though to pull it away from her mouth so that she would speak . . .'

'You must be steady . . .'

'And the finger broke off with a brittle snap and something clear welled from the stump . . .'

'You see clearly . . .'

'And from the broken finger I held something seeped in long shining strings and I knew it was honey, and half meaning it and half not I crammed the finger into my mouth . . .'

'More and more relaxed . . .'

'. . . and I tasted it and it was heavenly and I swung round to all our people and I shouted out, "Oh, Madame — she is delicious!"'

'Calmer and calmer . . .'

'And they came out of their rows, out of their seats, tumbling up on to the stage all in their velvets like an avalanche of bees, all plucking and picking at Madame who crumbled and dwindled so that in thirty seconds I swear . . .'

'Deep and calm, deep and calm, breathe . . .'

'There was no Madame. She had gone so fast that not a crumb of wax or drop of honey was left, so fast that none was spilt, not on the boards, not on her strewn clothes, which were left like the empty husk of a bee on the stage. I found that I held in my hand the veiling shawl of her wings. I let it fall, and it settled with her other things. I looked round and saw everybody smiling with an inward look at that heavenly taste, and I looked inward and tasted and knew I should never lose the memory of it, which was soaking into my very marrow as it faded from my tongue. I looked again at my fellow beekeepers and I saw on their faces too the mounting horror as they realised that they had loved nothing so much in their lives — no, not the song, not the teaching, as . . . ah . . .'

'Deeper and stronger, breathe deeply . . .'

'. . . as sinking my teeth into that fragile comb which burst into my mouth with delirious sweetness, and that I was freed from my rival for ever . . .'

'Breathe, deep and deeper . . .'

'. . . but never free of her memory, her meaning. She was gone for ever, yet she was not gone. Like the Jack-in-the-Box that is taller than what locks it in, she had sprung, as it were, everywhere; she was present by her sacrifice everywhere, like radio; not only an inextinguishable memory, but in literal fact taken into our bodies, walking with our legs, behind our faces, witnessing the flavour of our love-making, travelling between our legs in the honeys we exchanged out of our bodies, sweetening the acts of our wombs, sweetening the very juice the floating unborn baby drank. She was like a conception we had thrust into ourselves, that would take its form in our bodies and behaviours; we would do as she would do, dress as she would, treat the patients and pupils that came to us as she would, teach as she wanted. It was as if I had swallowed the font of honey itself, the benevolence. How could I be myself, how could I know my own spirit or the age of my ghost filled with this universal one! deep within me, swelling with her unendurable sweetness. Yet the crime must be concealed for ever, for else this Institute would be destroyed, where she compels within us that her work must go on for ever . . .'

'Your face is wet. Your eyes have begun to open, your skin has relented, it is pouring tears and sweat, you are dwindling as I watch; why Daniel, you are swimming in your own juices, your greases, they are overflowing and slopping on the floor.'

I whisked off the dove-grey coverlet, which was strangely darkened with spreading maps of Ireland. The body underneath was perfectly proportioned, except that the little man's erection made me feel like a dwarf. My hand was wet with his tears and I touched it to my mouth. The taste startled me. It was like a magnificent honey with a bitter spiritous undertaste, as if it had been laced with rum. I helped the tiny man to his feet, and bending in a way which put a considerable strain on my back, put my arm around his shoulders and marched him into the next room, the one with the broken mirror. His proudly angled staff preceded him, like Punch riding on his donkey.

He stood looking angrily at the sheeted mirror.

'Has somebody died?' he said.

'Yes,' I replied, 'but now you can endure to know it. Madame is dead.'

He pulled the sheet off the mirror, and stood staring at his splendid endowment. The crack that had split his image was missing. I reasoned that the nurse must have had the mirror changed while we were busy. But in that case, why had she sheeted it? I had suggested this only to conceal the flaw.

'Madame dead? What nonsense! She is upstairs.'

'That's your way of speaking, I know. But there's no need to pretend to me now. Her spirit and her work will always be with us.'

'Aren't you a patient here?'

'I am one of your fellow-facilitators.'

'No you're not. You're a loony, and you're making things up.'

'Well, if I was, it certainly did you no harm.' I was looking at that extraordinary organ, which throbbed slightly, as though on wings of air.

'I can't help that. I shall certainly report you to Madame if you go on spreading these slanderous rumours. It will go on your card.'

I didn't mind this. He was so beautifully hung. Her throat full in the open lily-wings of her nurse's uniform, Cecilia evidently thought so too, for she bent and kissed its tip, then kneeled.

'Will you leave now, Mr Donald, or Mr Derek, whichever you are?' said Daniel, not taking his eyes off Cecilia's profile; 'you will find a complaint on your docket in due course.'

As I put my hand to the door, the nurse continued her nursing work. She looked up at me with her mouth full, and winked.

* * * * *

I was in the bee-loud garden with Sir Geoffrey. As usual he was, like the night-sky, sky-clad.

'Do you see,' he said, 'men find all their gods too dangerous. They must be torn to pieces. We cannot endure that the god should walk among us whole. Yet, having torn, we mourn their absence, hoping they will return. We resent both presence and absence in Them. But why was our goddess so strong, and yet so weak, so prepared to disappear? Yet it is perhaps what she had to teach. Listen. Do you not hear? The Mistress is still in the flowers, travelling with the bees, assembling into the hives. Sweetness and light gather for another assault; the honey gathers until it is too heavy, and the hive of heaven cannot hold it. Listen to her, to her song, she is putting herself together, until the next time, the next place.'

'The next trial.'

'Was it a trial? We of the Institute have been facilitated, have become what we are; and it wasn't always quite what we expected or wanted, brushed by these wings.'

'Was Madame the only achieved one among them? Has she left behind nothing but mourners and impersonators? Daniel, that monster!'

'We've only got his word for that! And the impersonators are instructed to deny that they are imitations. Don't forget, the question of where Madame is still remains open. It is the policy. Mine was only one opinion. Count the blessings you have seen and felt. One found how to cross his dangerous threshold without losing awareness, and found beyond it a person he did not have to make out of himself; Donald found his purpose imprinted upon him by the skin of a woman; and it was he, or Derek, who found in himself the patience of a healer; another made his great confession and found that he was after all devoted to women.

Any of them would now be ready for marriage with Madame, or some other woman.'

'Who is to marry Madame, then? Do you mean dying?'

'That depends where Madame really is.'

'I wanted to marry her.'

'I know you did, Donald.'

'My name is Derek!' I swallowed my annoyance, and continued. 'What did you get out of your years here, Geoffrey?'

Now it was his turn to look cross.

'Don't you like my poetry at all?'

I looked at him warmly.

'Of course I do. Especially the way you write it.'

'Madame loved that,' he said, 'it made her laugh aloud. I was her lover for a while, you know.'

Did he realise that I had slept with Madame – or hadn't, if Daniel's confession was true?

'She said that I was the only man she knew who had two colours of ink in my pen. One was, she said, for reading about the night in the daytime. The other ink that came from me, she said, wrote luminous personal messages between her two big toes.'

'Are you sure it was Madame?'

'She was not allowed to admit that she was not,' he said, rather haughtily. 'Have you been to the church?'

'No, I didn't realise there was one. Not in this Institute.'

'It is for people who have grown tired of their own imaginations, or who want white weddings. Through the arch, to the North.'

I crossed the lawn between the hives, and went through the arch in the old stone wall. To be sure, there was a smallish church beyond, that looked old enough to have been here considerably longer than the Institute. The gravestones were more abundant than I would have expected from some chapel on private land. Many were quite new. Wandering among them, I came upon a curious feature. Where the inscription is usually carved, one of the stones had a long metal mirror riveted to its front. It was a very old stone, but the mirror was polished silvery-bright. Small, in the bottom right-hand corner, there was a name, engraved in cursive script like good handwriting. I bent to read it. *D. D. Holliday,* it said. There were no dates. As I straightened up, I inspected my reflection in the mirror. Yes, I looked no younger than my forty-six years; but I was in reasonable shape, and looked no older either. Just then a young woman in grey suit and frilly blouse came round the corner of the church. There was a big clear puddle in her way, and she picked round it carefully. Then she looked up and saw me, and smiled. I recognised her! It was Cecilia, and I couldn't for the life of me see how it could be.

* * * * *

I unlocked the little cupboard in the skirting-board where the tap was hidden, and started to turn it off. Xavier tried to see by the way my belly hung when I bent whether I was pregnant yet. The whispering in Aristotle's head dwindled and stopped. They all stood around me, watching, waiting for my decision, Xavier, Daniel, Geoffrey, Derek and Donald. I wondered whether I should tell them that the man I had chosen stood quietly among them, watching the silent head become dull as the water no longer ran over it.

'Will you tell us now, Madame?' urged the most eager of the men, one of the many who thought he had deceived me in his purpose in coming to my Institute, but who had deceived only himself, and that only for a little space. That one would find that he was not disappointed with what had happened here after all, though he was not to be my husband. Daniel the dwarf had almost won, with his intricate account of my death. Nice try, Daniel!

I would marry the one who had learnt to find his way in the dark, by a method which filled his pen and made me laugh aloud every time I thought about it. There he stood, black as night, called 'Sir' by mistake, yet it was an accurate nighthood. I turned the tap back on, and Aristotle started whispering again, whispering and shining. 'No,' I said, standing up and laughing through my veil, 'no, I'm afraid not. I think I'll wait a bit. This time I will be with you always. Greater works than these you will do. But I think I should like to hear a few more stories about me first.'

www.ingramcontent.com/pod-product-compliance
Lightning Source LLC
LaVergne TN
LVHW091004080826
845145LV00003B/1118

* 9 7 8 1 9 0 5 0 2 4 1 4 8 *